Glou

SHOE ON THE ROAD

A book of short stories

GLORIA DUPONT

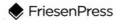 FriesenPress

One Printers Way
Altona, MB R0G 0B0
Canada

www.friesenpress.com

ISBN
978-1-0-915167-3 (Hardcover)
978-1-03-915166-6 (Paperback)
978-1-03-915168-0 (eBook)

1. FICTION, SHORT STORIES (SINGLE AUTHOR)

Distributed to the trade by The Ingram Book Company

SHOE ON THE ROAD

Stories in this series are:

Prologue

I am sure that many people who see shoes on the road, or a pair of shoes tied together and hanging on a wire, wonder how they happened to be there.

If shoes could talk, they could tell you the story. Some may be sad stories, or horror stories. Behind every shoe on the road there is a story.

Having been a storyteller since I was a child, I wanted to create some shoe stories to share. They are not all happy ever after stories.

Credits

I would like to thank my husband, Gerry, for encouraging me to check off my bucket list, and always being supportive.

I believe that as my family members read this they will think "*I know where she got that idea from*". Thank you very much to my family for contributing to my colorful imagination. If any of you are offended by the language that I use, please know that Phat Annie wrote those sentences.

Dedication

I would like to dedicate this book to our daughter Cindy. Always on our minds, forever in our hearts.

THE HIKING BOOT

.... behind every shoe on the road there is a story, this is one of them

The shoe was a brown hiking boot. Little toe and heel marks on the insole showed that the shoe had been worn a lot by a child, probably a boy about 6, with a high arch. There was a cut across the leather above the big toe, an old cut that looked like a knife mark, now filled with sand and dirt, cut nearly clear through.

The park was Constable Cardinal's territory; he had patrolled it every working day for the last year. This was his first assignment out of RCMP Academy in Regina, and he was proud of his progress. The other members of the RCMP had nicknamed him "Birdy" because he whistled when he was happy, and he was almost always whistling. They liked working with him and trusted him as a partner. He had grown up in this town, and stories are that things were tough for the family. The kids survived well, they worked hard in school, loved sports, and had lots of friends. It wasn't hard to believe because "Birdy" couldn't walk down the street today without a dozen people shouting greetings to him, and waving. He was handsome and friendly, and the ladies, young and old, loved him. Many of his sports teammates were still around town and would invite him to meet at the bar for a drink on a Friday night. He often went, but always drank Coke. He loved the camaraderie and bonding with the guys. There was no special lady in his life yet, who could blame him when all the ladies loved him. There was lots of time for getting serious and settling down.

The park was the meeting spot for drug sellers/buyers. The constable's size and manners were intimidating to the homeless drug users, but when he talked to them, he was kind, almost understanding. But Constable Cardinal was not on the job today. It was his birthday, July 16th, and he had taken the weekend off to enjoy water skiing on Okanagan Lake with his friends.

The police on the beat today listened to the witness's story and wrote everything down. There were children playing in the park, boys and girls, elementary school age. There was a football game in the park and the parents were in the stadium, allowing the little ones to go and play during half time – warned to return when the game resumed to watch their older brothers play. The witness was a middle-aged lady in the park alone on Saturday morning. She had phoned in on her cell to say that a man picked a little boy up, and she was afraid the boy had been abducted. The boy seemed to know the man who didn't say a word, he stopped the car on the road, and walked determinedly over to the lad, about 6, and grabbed him by the arm. The boy was kicking and screaming, "I'll tell my mom". The man forced him to the car, put him in the back seat, and drove away. The boys' soccer ball was left on the side of the road, the little hiking boot beside it. The other children were familiar with the boy, he lived near the park, and they had seen him last game, they didn't know his name. The other children were not from this district, some were siblings of the "visitor" team. They could describe the boy and the colors of his T-shirt and shorts, but they didn't remember his shoes.

Bobby loved camping. His Mom and Dad had taken him and his little brother on many camping trips from the time he could walk. His favorite thing was the campfire. Daddy would chop the wood, and Bobby would carry the kindling to the rocks. He would make a pyramid of the sticks, placing each one carefully the way Daddy had taught him. Often, they fell, and he would patiently start again. He wanted to strike the match, but Mommy said he was too little. When the fire was burning, he was allowed to poke at it with a long stick. This was his favorite time in the whole wide world. He wasn't even afraid of sleeping in the tent and listened for the sounds of the night. His father told him stories of his ancestors; how important the campfire was to them. Bobby loved his father very much, but his father left them and went to work in Vancouver. "Not your business" Mommy said, "but not your fault either".

After that, his mother still took them camping occasionally with Bobby's grandparents. It was never as much fun without his father, but Grandpa was a good companion too. Grandpa said Bobby was getting to be a big boy and could use the hatchet to cut some wood. Grandpa carefully supervised him, and he got some splinters off the big block with his little hatchet and carried them to the fire.

One weekend his father came to visit. His mother and father were getting along well, and Daddy said, "Let's go camping, I miss that the most." His parents started out having fun, then they spent a lot of time talking loudly, and yelling. It got worse when they started drinking beer. Bobby hated beer. Bobby thought if he showed Daddy what a big boy he was now, they would be happier. He looked for the hatchet, and then he remembered that it was in Grandpa's gear. He walked over to the wood stack. His father's axe was there stuck in a block. Bobby pulled it out gently. He had no idea how heavy it would be. He tried to hold it up, but down it went, right through Bobby's hiking boot. His toes hurt, and he hollered for Mommy.

His parents rushed toward him, Daddy grabbed the axe and Mommy grabbed Bobby. She removed his boot, fearing what she would see. His big toe was nicked and hardly bleeding, it would be very bruised. Then his father started yelling that his mother was irresponsible, and this is what the boys were becoming, and lots of nasty stuff. And his father yelled at him. "Buck up, Bobby, big boys don't cry!" he said. They packed up and went home.

Bobby didn't see much of his father after that. Bobby knew it was his entire fault no matter what Mommy said. She drank a lot of beer after that, and both Bobby and his younger brother Jimmy spent as much time at the school playground and at the park as they could to avoid being sad for Mommy.

The hiking boot with the cut remained to be Bobby's favorite shoe; he wore the boots everywhere even in the summer.

Constable Cardinal returned to work Monday morning, tanned, and beaming, and whistling up a storm. His brother had come down from C.F.B. Edmonton where he was a soldier in training. Funny that both the Cardinal boys would end up carrying guns. He thought the first thing to do was to get caught up on what happened on his beat.

Mrs. Weinberg had phoned in on her cell phone to report an abduction on Saturday morning. The busy body was on the job again; she figured park watch was her responsibility. Just being a good citizen perhaps. Last week she had told him that she saw someone stalking him, a lady, about her age, peeking around buildings at him.

Norah Weinberg's life was a calm one. She would go to the park every weekday morning and watch her soaps in the afternoon. HE spent all his time at the store, and she wasn't wanted there. They never had children because the store sucked all the fluid out of the man. They were rich enough to buy a new home in a subdivision, but he liked to be near downtown so he could walk to the store. Norah usually only went to the park on weekdays, but this Saturday was such a beautiful day that she couldn't resist taking a walk. She loved the park, even though it was where druggies slept in the woods, they were never around in the morning. Weekends brought school aged children and football games, and rowdies. Weekdays were quieter, and she would watch the mothers with their toddlers. She could have adopted, she often thought she should just take one of those cute little kids home with her, their mothers didn't watch them closely enough. Some of them probably didn't even want their kids. Norah thought a little boy would have been best, because she wasn't a cookie baking, lace sewing, fluffy woman. She preferred to hoe the planters and prune the trees.

The park needed more attendants, so Norah was on watch to see that nothing illegal happened when she was there. Hadn't she reported the flower cutters, the kids who fed the ducks cheezies, the lad who left the doggie deposit on the grass and the teens who must have been playing hooky? Just last week she used her cell phone to tell Constable Cardinal about the woman who seemed to be stalking him. Peeking around the biffy building, watching him. He thanked her and told her she was very helpful in the park. She could have had a son just like him. She would have named him Aaron after her father.

When she saw the young boy grabbed and shoved into the car, she didn't panic at all, she just picked up her cell phone and called the station. She had it on her speed dial. Constable Cardinal was not in, it was Saturday, and a policewoman was put on the line. She told her about the abduction, and the lady Constable came right to the park and took notes, and asked all the children around for details, and really covered the investigation well. She took down the color and shape of the car and would bring pictures for Norah to look at later. She thanked Norah for being a good citizen, and Norah felt so good about the day that she thought she might walk to the store and tell Him about it. Boy, if that had been her boy, he wouldn't have been snatched so easily.

Constable Cardinal read the reports on the abduction with concern. "Any reports of a missing child in town?" He asked the dispatcher. "None at all, that is funny, eh? A boy was reported as grabbed in the park and taken away in a car, but there are no boys reported missing. Some mother is sure going to regret not keeping tabs on her child." Well, thought Cardinal, some mothers have a hard time of it. I remember straying away from home myself, usually with Jimmy though, and things were different when we were kids, we didn't even think of being taken. Things were tough for our mother.

Cardinal's mother, Anne was a small-town girl. She fell head over heels in love with Ab Cardinal the day she met him. He was tall, dark, handsome as all get out, and had a JOB.

They had two baby boys and life was good. Somehow things changed when the boys were toddlers; perhaps she cared more for the boys than for Ab. Perhaps she forgot that he needed attention too. The best times were when they went out camping, Ab was an outdoorsman. He could have taught the boys so much if he had stayed around. He loved to hunt and trap and knew so many stories of his family in the old days when they lived off the land. Anne did not like guns or hunting or eating wild meat, her boys had none of that.

After Ab left, things were ok as long as he sent money for the rent and groceries. But after a while he stopped sending support, and Anne had no idea where he was. She started using some of the welfare money for a case of beer or two. When you are lonely a nice cold drink helps ease things, makes life seen less difficult.

The boys started being ashamed of her. Anne reasoned that she couldn't afford nice dresses, and she never was a good housekeeper. They never brought their friends home or asked her to come to the school events.

Anne met Paul in the bar. He was good to her, and the boys didn't need her anymore. They were wasting time in high school when they could be out getting jobs and helping to pay for their keep. Both boys did work some after school and in the summer, but they could be bringing in full time wages. They would be fine without her, and Paul needed a companion to make his life more enjoyable on the road. A trucker's life is lonely, and he would take real good care of her. They had so much in common, they even liked the same kind of beer.

Anne tried to keep track of her boys, and never forgot their birthdays. It was more important to her than Christmas because everyone could remember Christmas. July 16th. September 30. Important days to Anne. She would mail birthday cards to her mom, who still lived in her hometown and saw the boys often.

Paul hadn't worked out, it was ok for a few years, but she got tired of his bullshit. He thought he owned her. She didn't even want to remind herself of how she survived after that, but she did survive. No matter where she went, or how lightly she traveled, her backpack with her life's memories went with her. This year the bag seemed a bit heavy, and she thought she would lighten her load. The wedding picture of her and Ab she left at her mothers. She thought she could stay there awhile, but her mother had got to be old and crotchety. Thought she could tell her what to do and wouldn't allow a drink in her house. Wouldn't give her a twenty so she could go to the bar.

The plastic toy soldier Jimmy had carried everywhere was in the backpack, and she thought she would try to get it to him this fall. She had already left a present for Bobby. The memory of her first-born was a reminder of the best times they ever had, a reminder of their camping trips and the campfires that warmed them all. Her backpack seemed lighter, but her heart was so heavy. She thought she just might find a ditch and lie down and die. Ab's damn ancestors would approve, they left old people behind to fend for themselves. Gave them food and water though, Ab had stopped sending the food a long time ago, he ruined her life and forgot about her and the boys.

Yes, thought Constable Cardinal, things were rough for his mother. He hadn't seen her for years and wondered if there would be a card in the mail for his birthday, she had never forgotten before - this was his only contact with her. He had better stop reminiscing and get back to work. "Where is the evidence?" he asked.

"In the 'evidence' room, Birdie" responded the dispatcher. "We are just waiting to see if any missing children are reported."

Cardinal found the file and the Ziploc with the little hiking boot inside. "Oh, my God" he whispered, "it's mine!" He held the little boot to his chest, tears welling down his high cheekbones. Thoughts tumbled through his mind: camping, kindling, Daddy, Pilsner, abandonment. The Cardinal brothers, Jimmy and Bobby, swimming upstream and making a life for themselves. *She must have been in town*, he thought. His mother was here and didn't have the nerve to meet with him. *I bet that was the lady Mrs. Weinberg saw hiding behind buildings and stalking me in the park. Damn her alcoholic being."* he thought. *"Buck up, Bobby,"* he told himself, *"Big boys don't cry"*.

"What do you think, Cardinal?" the dispatcher asked.

"Well, I think that there was no abduction, or kidnapping at all. When I was a kid, I ran off to the park all the time. I think what happened was an old busy body, Mrs. Weinberg, minding everyone's business, reported a father. A father, who was ticked off at his son r⸴ ⸴nⸯng to the park on a Saturday morning without permission! ⸴d him back home to face the music. That's what I think. And ⸴s shoe, heck, smell it – it smells of tobacco and alcohol. No sweet smell of a little boy's foot, this boot hasn't been worn for years. Who knows how it got to the curbside, who cares!" Bobby Cardinal practically choked on the last words, *"I care Mom, thank you for the birthday present. Thank you for my life,"* he thought.

MITTENS AND KITTENS

...behind every shoe on the road there is a story, and this is one of them

The old man's screams could be heard down the hall at the nursing station. Night shift nurse, Mary, raced to room 102 and threw open the door. She hurried to the bedside and put her arms around the old man. "Harold, it is Mary, are you ok? Was it the nightmare again?"

"Mitten on the road, Mary, oh my god there was a mitten on the road. It was so horrible, and I got so scared. The brown eyes were staring at me." Harold sobbed. He was shaking and wet with perspiration from his night sweats.

"I will get you some tea, Harry, and we will get you into a nice dry pair of warm pajamas." Mary helped Harry to the La-Z-Boy chair in his room. It had a nice homemade quilt lying on it. She wrapped him in the blanket and asked if he would be ok while she went to get the pajamas and tea. "Just relax in this nice quilt your daughter Jessica made for you and I will be right back."

Harry calmed down, he knew he could count on Mary to come back quickly and take care of him. He hadn't wanted to move into the senior citizens home, but his girls had their own families, and they were so busy running a taxi service getting their kids to school and games and lessons. When he was a kid, he walked to and from school and to everything around town; he couldn't understand why kids who needed exercise had to be driven to everything. He missed his wife Ester so much, but he had got used to being alone again. Time heals a lot of hurts and makes some just a little easier to remember. But some things would never go away, would never be eased, and would never stop giving him nightmares. The mitten on the road was one of them.

His brothers had gone off to the Second World War, but Harry didn't go because he was too young, and someone had to help their father with the farm work. "Someone needs to feed those boys, Harry," his father would say "So don't worry, you are doing your part for the war effort too. We will all do our part."

Harry finished grade 10, if you could say that -he missed most of the fall classes and all the spring classes. He stayed on the farm after that, and he and his father fought droughts, floods, pests, grasshoppers, and rocks that kept rising to the topsoil. Grains took care of themselves in the summer, but there was always something to do. He learned to repair machinery, sharpen tools, and because they also had milk cows the work was never done. At harvest time all hell broke loose. Hired help was sought for the harvest. Mother fed the crew two meals a day, so she also needed help. In 1944, she hired a girl named Ester. Perhaps she was plain, but Harry didn't think so, he loved the way she flicked her long hair, and she smelled so clean, and laughed like a bubbling brook. At coffee time, his mother and Ester would bring the old pickup truck to the field with hot coffee and cinnamon buns. Ester's hair was the color of wheat, her cheeks the color of roses, and Harry turned red when she talked to him. Harry was hooked.

Wedding dances were a huge community event back then, everyone would whirl around the floor doing polkas and waltzes to a live band, even the little children would be out dancing. The men would bid on boxed lunches, and Harry would cheat. He would make sure he knew which one was Ester's and bid on it until he won so that he could sit with her and share the lunch. Well past midnight, the children would be asleep on coats on the benches, and things would be winding down. Some men would be outside swilling drinks out of the flask from their hip pocket. Harry would be getting up enough nerve to take Ester home in the old farm pick-up.

Two of his brothers came back home: one did not. The war had changed them, and they brought their own demons home with them. A grenade had killed his brother, Harry didn't want to hear any more details about the death, and he couldn't believe that someone had intentionally taken the life out of his brother. For the first time Harry was relieved that he wasn't old enough to fight, he didn't think he could have stood killing a man, seeing the bleeding and loss of limbs and all the wounded men. He didn't think he could inflict a wound on another human being. Oh sure, he fought with his brothers all his life, punching, and wrestling and rolling on the ground. They used to get into trouble for fighting in the bales and scaring the cows and he had no end to the stories he could tell on his brothers. But to maim, to disfigure, to kill, this he could not stomach. His brothers slept in the bunkhouse, and sometimes Harry would hear one of them yell out in his sleep, reliving the horror of the battles. Harry would get shivers down his spine and hope that his brother would soon forget and find peace again. He would think of the waves on the wheat field, or Ester 's smile so he could go to sleep again.

Mr. and Mrs. Harold Rand got married by a Justice of the Peace on a beautiful Saturday afternoon in 1947. The wedding dance was a huge success, people were relieved the war was ended, and were ready to celebrate again. They got their own little piece of land, a little house, a dog, and started their life together. It didn't take them many years to outgrow the house with two girls and two boys filling the house with screams and laughter. Farming was tough, their land not very productive, and it was hard to feed and school the family. Ester wanted her girls to go to school, not quit in grade nine and hire out to help farm women do the chores. She wanted her boys to get an education and a career and not to become farmers like generations of men in the family before them.

Harry loved farming, wanted his kids to run free in the fields and fish at the stream. But he lost heart on the day of the accident.

Gus was a good horse, had pulled the stone boat many miles. Content to pull on ahead, he had hauled the plow, the seeder, the thresher, the sugar wagon, and the sleigh. He and Harry had worked the land side by side as hard as they could. Always steady, always strong. Neither of them knew the barbed wire fence was there. Gus was harnessed and ready to go, they were pulling deadfall out of the woods. This would be cut and split for firewood and burned in the wood stove this winter. "Ha!" yelled Harry flicking the reins, Gus grunted and pulled the log, and then Gus stumbled and fell. Harry dropped the reins and rushed forward; Gus was struggling to get up. There was a hole in the ground where the post of the fence used to be. The post was rotten and lying at a 45-degree angle, the barbed wire stretched from there to a tree nearby. Gus had stumbled into the hole, fallen forward and the barbed wire had cut into his forefoot as he fell. Harry felt the pain with Gus and knew that this was the end for his buddy; a horse with a broken leg was done. He had to get into action immediately, starting by running to the farmhouse. Yelling to David and Harry Jr. as he jumped into the pickup, he drove as fast as he could to his brother's farm. His brother would have to come and shoot Gus, as Harry could not do this. It was not that he was squeamish or couldn't stand the sight of blood. Harry delivered baby calves, he assisted many cows by reaching into the birth canal and turning a calf that was sideways or breach so that it could be delivered safely. He had lanced a pus-filled growth on a cat's head and let it drain. He had put salve on many cuts and scrapes on livestock's legs. Hell, he had even neutered pets and livestock, but he could not kill. Once a cat had crawled into the warm hood of the truck on a cold winter day. When Harry started the truck, the cat was nearly severed in two by the fan belt and spun out onto the ground. Ester had taken a rock and finished off the cat because Harry could not do it. Ester butchered the chickens for Sunday dinner. Harry's brother would come and cull out the runt piglets from the litter, the squealers, because Harry could not kill them. Ester used to tease him about insects and mice, but she didn't mean anything, she knew her man loved too much and valued life too much to take it away from anything.

The Rands didn't protect their children from the facts of life, or the circle of life, but they softened it for them. Driving into town they would often see a dead cat, rabbit, deer, or dog on the road. Ester would say "Harry, be careful there is a shoe on the road." And Harry would swerve around the roadkill. Or "Oh, no, there is another mitten on the road, we've seen a lot of that this spring haven't we!" commenting on their loss of wild rabbits to the increasing traffic on the roads. After a while Catherine and Jessica caught on, and they would declare that there was a mitten on the road. You should have seen the looks on the faces of Harry and Ester the first time one of the girls said it. The couple looked at each other in surprise and smiled. They were busted.

The death of Gus bothered his owner very much. After his brother had shot Gus, Harry had to help with the body. The leg had bled from the barbed wire cut, and a bone was splintered in the leg. Harry avoided looking at the bullet shot between Gus's huge brown eyes. Ester said later, "I think you loved that old horse as much as you love me!" "Maaaaybe", Harry teased. Harry gave up on the farm at that point; Ester thought he just couldn't do it alone without Gus. He reasoned that the land wasn't producing enough to support his family, so in 1962 Harry got a job in town, driving a truck for Shell Oil. Harry's job was to pick up fuel in the city and deliver it to farmer's yards. He would return to their small town at night with stories of this farmer or that, and how the crops were growing, and what baby livestock was born in the spring. He hadn't left the farm - he was just not fighting it anymore. The kids liked living in town, they could get involved in sports after school and visit their friends. Now that the girls were teenagers, Ester got a part time job at the Dollar Store to put away money for college, no options - the kids were going. Things were going well for the Rand family.

In the city, Allan Caruthers was growing up. This year, 1972, he had just turned twelve and got his first job delivering the Journal. It was a tough job, as Allan had to get up and out of the house by 5:00 every morning, go to the paper shack to pick up his papers, and then walk to the 43 houses around his neighborhood and be finished in time to return home, have breakfast with his parents and little sister, and then off to school which started at 9:00. That meant that bedtime was about 8 p.m. It wasn't so bad in the fall when he first started, but it was getting cold, and mornings in Northern Alberta can be very cold.

Allan was an easygoing lad with dark curly hair, and big brown eyes. He was sturdily built, and in good shape, so the walk was not a problem for him. It was lonely out there in the morning. He would be at most houses before the families were up, there would be a light on here and there, people stirring to go to work. Some men would be out warming up their vehicle, and they would greet Allan on their driveways. He loved animals and knew every outdoor dog on the route. He didn't have a lot of time, but there was always time for a pat on the head, or a neck scratch for the puppies. Allan was growing up in the days before cell phones, but this was a friendly neighborhood, and his parents felt he was safe out there. The biggest danger was that he had to cross a truck route to get to the paper shack, the pickup spot, but there generally was very little traffic around five in the morning. He was doing this for the money. Allan wanted a new bicycle, a new ball glove, and skates. He had asked for them for Christmas, but never got what he wanted. He got clothes for Christmas, and for birthdays. He knew their family had to budget, and if the kids needed new clothes, it was practical to combine necessity with gift giving. He did also get puzzles and stuff, but didn't anyone see the need for Allan to have a ball glove? One Grandma gave him slippers, and the other gave him books. He had already read every Hardy Boy book ever written. Allan was very bright in school and whizzed through all his work so that he could read. He loved writing and was thinking of being a journalist and writing about sports. That way he could go to all the big games for free!!

It was bitterly cold this January morning, probably 30 below, Allan thought. There was freezing wind and blowing snow. Allan pulled his parka hood up over his head (his little sister called it his "hoobin") and hoisted his Journal bag over his shoulder. The Journal must be delivered. Yesterday he had listened to the Super Bowl game with his father on the radio. Their black and white TV only had two channels and didn't carry the game. Dallas Cowboys played Miami Dolphins. Boy, that was quite a game for Dallas. Allan would one day cover the Super Bowl; he was thinking about how he would have written up Staubach's first touchdown. And then how he would have described the quarterback Staubach throwing the ball for a touchdown in the 4th. Quarter as he passed 7 yards to Ditka for the last touchdown and Dallas's first Super Bowl Championship. He would make the game exciting even though the Dolphins were totally dominated and conjure up a picture for the person reading his article like Ray Scott, the radio announcer, did for him. Head down, hood pulled well down over his forehead, he slugged along in the freezing cold, deep in thought.

"Visibility is very poor this morning, and the roads are icy. Drivers out there please take caution as the blowing snow is making things very hard to see on the road. We have blizzard conditions here folks", the radio announcer warned.

"Boy, you can say that again" thought Harry Rand who was on his way out of the city after filling his gas tank for today's deliveries. The truck route had very little activity at this time of the morning, he was thankful for that. Harry had almost missed the red light at the intersection; it wasn't until he was almost at the crossroad when he saw the light. "*I should just turn around and park this rig, no farmer is going to need gas today anyway. But today is the day I deliver to the Hutterite colony, and I would mess up next week if I didn't do that today. The gas must be delivered*", he thought. There was a curve in the road up ahead, he knew this road by heart, so he didn't have to slow down to make it. As he entered the curve – bang! "What the" Harry sputtered; he thought he had hit something. He slowed to a stop as quickly as he could and got out of the truck to look things over. There was a snow boot on the road. A real snow boot on the road. There was a figure lying almost in the ditch, "Oh my God, I did hit something" Harry rushed to the figure; it was a child, a child in a parka. Near him was a Journal Paper shoulder bag. Harry's stomach lurched, and fear gripped his heart. He bent over the child, whose face was a mass of blood. He felt for warm breath at his nose. He looked at the crumpled body, and then he buckled and puked on the road. A car stopped and the gentleman came over to Harry. "Any trouble Mister" he asked, and then realized the driver was humped over a body. "Call the police," yelled Harry "and get an ambulance."

It seemed to take forever for the ambulance and police to get there. Harry finally heard sirens, and shortly thereafter saw red lights looking furry in the blowing snow. Harry had taken his coat off and put it over the boy "I'm sorry, I'm so so sorry, God help me. Live, please don't die on me, please, I didn't kill you, please live!" Harry thought the boy was still alive, but he was looking down into lifeless big brown eyes, and there was no movement at all. He stroked the boy's black curly hair wet with blood, like he would a kitten, a kitten on the road.

The paramedics put the lad on a stretcher, picked up his bag, and rolled him to the ambulance. One of them put a blanket around Harry, who hadn't noticed that he was freezing, and a policeman guided him to the police car, Harry's coat over his arm. Because Harry was so upset, the policeman called Shell Oil, who sent another driver out to drive the fuel truck back to the station. Before they left the scene, Harry cried, "the boot, there is a boot on the road, the boy will need that." The policeman tried to be gentle, but he didn't know how he could soften the blow of the words, "The boy was not breathing, Sir, the paramedic pronounced him dead." Then the policeman drove Harry home.

Ester ran to the door to greet her husband and the policeman. "Harry, oh, Harry, are you hurt? What happened?" "A mitten" Harry sobbed, "a mitten on the road!" "I am afraid he is very confused ma'am, there was an accident, your husband hit a child on the truck route." "Is he?" "Yes" said the policeman, "I am afraid so. You should call a doctor. Your husband needs something to help him."

Ester cut the article about the accident out of the Journal. She also saved the obituary. She thought Harry might want to know about it someday, but she hid it well so that it could not be found. Harry never asked.

Harry continued to drive the fuel truck for another 20 years. But he never was the same. The kids were already grown up when the accident had happened; the boys were in college at the time. Ester helped him through the tough months; she was his strength, his saving grace, and his angel. Harry retired the day he was 65, in 1992. He told Ester that he would like to move back to the farm, Ester said she would think about it, but Ester didn't know then that she would not live beyond that year. Harry had lost so many loved ones throughout his life, and the sorrow was extreme, but none of those deaths carried sadness as deep as the accident. Harry couldn't talk about it; he could only dream about it – and those dreams are called nightmares!

The children all got an education like their mother planned. Jessica and Catherine got married and had grandchildren for Harry and they carried on their mother's tradition when they saw roadkill. The boys thought it was rather silly; a dead cat was a dead cat.

Mary came back to Room 102 with the tea and warm pajamas. Harry was slumped in the chair, head forward, he must have fallen asleep. She walked over to him and put a hand on his shoulder. "Harry, I have tea. Harry" No response. Mary stood back a bit and studied him, and then felt for a pulse. There was none. *Harry had been a dear old soul. What was the demon, she wondered, that haunted him at night? How could a mitten on the road scare such a strong-minded man? A mitten … brown eyes…? What was Harry's story?* she wondered.

THE RED SPIKED HEEL

Fraser, Alicia Marie

Alicia passed away suddenly and unexpectedly in Kelowna on May 24, 2009, at the age of 35 years. She will be sadly missed by her loving family: sons Bradley (12) and Darren (15), her mother Elizabeth Duran and her friend Matthew Seaton. Donations can be sent to the Salvation Army. A private family service was held following cremation.

There it was in black and white, a simple announcement to tell the world that Alicia was free. She would no longer have to suffer the cold nights on the street, the seductive call of the love of her life, the humiliation of having to work for strange men, the pain in her heart when she thought of her sons, the wanton feelings, the desperation, the loneliness when in a crowd, living in a loveless relationship. She was free. Alicia had been cremated as per her wish; she always said, "Why wait to burn in hell when it can be done in your own hometown." *Was she the only one that was set free, or did her death give all who knew her the freedom from guilt, regret, and helplessness?* " Although most of our memories were unspeakable and hurt too much to share, some of us spoke about Alicia at her memorial,

Bradley: "I am sad that my mother is dead. In the last 4 years I didn't get to see her very much, mostly on our birthdays and Christmas and other holidays at Grandma's house. I never visited her where she lived, so I don't know what that was like. When I was little Darren and I lived with Mommy. I can remember her playing in the back yard with us and cheering us on when we did tricks on the trampoline. She liked to cook hamburger dishes, and her Sloppy Joes were my favorites. Mommy loved animals and we had cats ever since I can remember. She told me that Spike used to sleep in my crib when I was a baby, and she was never afraid that he would smother me. We had lots of toys and stuff. We would lay on the trampoline on starry nights, and she would make up stories about fairies and wishes and angels. My Mom believed that there were angels that looked after each of us on earth; they lived on earth until you died and then they were assigned to watch over someone else on earth. Each of us may have 4 or 5 angels guarding over us. She believed that we all come back to live again after we earned it by being an angel, and each time we become a person of higher value. I guess that is because we learn things when we are angels, but how can people be of different values, are we not equal? What did she mean? I wish I could ask her that now. I wish I could hug her again, and she could tell me how proud she was of me. I didn't love her enough these last years, if I had loved her more maybe she would still be alive now, it was just that as months went by, I knew her less and less, and she hardly knew me anymore – she still thought I was a little boy and couldn't relate to my stories of school and friends and stuff. Where were her angels the day she died, why didn't they protect her from a horrible death?"

Darren: "The last year when we lived with Mom was not an easy one for me. I remember setting my alarm to get myself up for school. I would go to Mom's room, and she would be sound asleep, her mascara smeared on her cheeks, still dressed – sometimes even still had her boots on. I would push on her arm and call her, but she wouldn't wake up. Sometimes she wasn't even home yet. I would go to Bradley's room and see that he was up and dressed, then try to find something for our breakfast. Often there wasn't any bread or anything, but there was a can of Ravioli or something, so we would eat that before school. Sometimes we went to school without breakfast and had no lunch to take. We would tell our friends or teacher that we had forgotten our lunch and often someone would share with us. Sometimes we had money and walked to the corner store for lunch stuff.

Mom started selling and then we had lots of money. She showed me how she had pulled the toilet paper holder out of the drywall and the board between the wood made a shelf. She had little bags of white stuff on the shelf, and a draw string bag filled with money. She said that if anything happened to her, I was to take the bag of money for us boys. I know she was snorting the powder, but she never did it in front of us. She would go into the bathroom and come out high, sometimes with a residue of powder on her upper lip, and then she would leave the house. One day a big, tattooed guy came to the house and he and Mom started yelling at each other. She sent us to our rooms, but we could still hear. He wanted the money she owed for the stuff she sold, if there wasn't enough money, he said she must be using too much. He threatened to hurt her badly if she didn't get the money. The next day the bike that Grandma bought me for my birthday went missing from the front hall. Mom said someone must have broken into the house and taken it and didn't want to report to the police. There was also a big dent in the side of her car that she didn't want to explain to us. I thought then that she must be involved with the Hell's Angels or something.

Shortly after that mom boarded up the family room. She said we were going to get rich soon and not to worry about the threats, as someone was going to help her now. It was spring break and she sent us boys to our Grandparents for the holiday, because Grandma, being a teacher, had spring break also. After the holidays I kept bugging her to show me what was in the family room, so one day she showed me. There were about a hundred little plants on tables and bright lights and fans overhead, she said friends helped her get started and we would get rich from the first crop – but it was a secret and I had to swear not to tell anyone. It was a couple of months after that when our house was raided by the police, and we moved to live with Grandma .

I have been angry with Mom for the last four years. She abandoned Bradley and me. We were doing fine when she was working at the plant. I know it was hard work, but we had a house, a car, food, and everything we needed. We weren't the best dressed kids at school, but we are boys and didn't care much about that. Mom had some boy friends, but they were mostly nice guys. I see now that the trouble started when she started going out with Shaun, and that is when she started to miss work and stopped being there for us. Often when we came home from school Mom and Shaun would be on the couch and they were high. And then when he stopped coming around things got worse for her, she got fired etc. That is when she started going out at night.

I missed home for the first while, but Brad and I had a good home with our Grandmother. She was, and still is always there for us, helping us with homework, going to our games, welcoming our friends. But that made me angrier at Mom, she should be doing these things for us, she should be caring for us. Instead, she dumped us and went out on the street. I haven't told you guys, but I saw her one night when my friend and I went to the show. We had to walk a couple of blocks from the theatre to catch the bus, and there were three women standing on the street corner. I was mortified when I saw that one was Mom. My friend made some lewd jokes and said too bad we spent our money on the show; we could have hired a hooker. Mom started talking to a guy through the passenger door of a car, and then got in. Thank goodness she did because I didn't know what I was going to do if we walked right past my mom. I still see her there in my mind, she was dressed in a leather halter and tight blue jeans, and she had red spiked high heels on and a bag that matched. Mom was really a beautiful lady; I should have been proud to introduce her to my friend. Did she see me? I will never know.

I know I haven't done well for the last couple of years, school has slipped, and Grandma doesn't like some of my friends. I have made life miserable for my grandma, and I am sorry, but I just can't seem to be happy anymore. You think I don't appreciate you, but I love you and I will turn out ok, I'll get myself together, you'll see.

I am sorry, you guys, but Mom risked her own life. She didn't have to die this way; if she hadn't gotten in that fucking car, she would still be alive. She should have been at a decent job and off the drugs. She was smart and funny a few years ago, the last while she was paranoid and couldn't even stay in a conversation. She didn't even know Bradley and me anymore, she was hollow. Her hugs weren't even warm anymore. The only thing that was still my mom was that perfume, she wore the same kind ever since I can remember; if I close my eyes, I can smell it now. "Damn *you to hell bitch, you didn't try to get better, you didn't care anymore. You asked for this!*"

Elizabeth: "I am very saddened by the death of my daughter. I have a lot of regret, but I disposed of the mammoth load of guilt that I carried with me for so many years. I had to unload it, it was dragging me down, and I was drowning in it and had to pull myself free.

Alicia was a problem child from the hours of difficult labour to her last day. As a baby I carried her on my hip for hours trying to ease her colic. She was a very smart and intelligent girl and excelled in elementary school. As a teen she tested me every inch of the way. She wanted to wear revealing clothing to school, wanted to run with the gang, tested alcohol, tested drugs, and tested her authorities at school. I tried to reason with her, threaten her, ground her, punish her, reward her, but never did find the clue to success as her parent. I was so proud that she graduated from high school; she just scraped through because she never learned to study, but she did graduate. When she was finished school, she was expected to work but she had never learned to work. She shifted around and worked in bars and even worked as a stripper for awhile, and then the most incredible thing happened. She got pregnant.

I have never seen such a change in a person, such a complete turn around. Alicia quit smoking, quit taking all unhealthy substances, and got a job as a waitress. She maintained a small apartment and saved for baby things. She said she was the happiest she had ever been in her lifetime, she was going to have someone to love that was all hers, someone who would love her back. The father was a member of a travelling band, your father Darren and Bradley, and he came to Kelowna often."

Elizabeth looked directly at Darren. "Darren, you were the best thing that ever happened to your mom. You are very angry at your mother right now, and rightfully so, but you must forgive."

Elizabeth wiped the tears away and continued. "Alicia never did forgive her father for his relationship with her. Her father was an abusive person, and because he started to show this abuse towards Alicia, I came to my senses and divorced him. This happened just as she was becoming a teen, therefore part of the problem of bringing up Alicia. She told me years later that he abused her sexually. I have a hard time believing that is true because I never saw any sign of it, but why would she make up such a terrible thing? She said she hated him, and because of that you boys have never met her father, we have not communicated with him since the day she told me why she was so bitter towards him. *Am I responsible to tell him that Alicia has passed away? It is too soon; I must think about that*, she thought.

Three years after Darren was born, another blessing occurred, and Alicia had another one to love with the birth of Bradley. With two little ones, Alicia stayed at home. She got assistance from Welfare and seemed to manage on it. She tried to be the best Mother she could be and took good care of the boys. When Bradley started walking, she got the job at the plant and did very well as an employee there. She got promoted to a supervisory job, rented a nice house with a back yard close to schools, bought a car, and life was good.

Alicia dated a few guys, and really did want to get married. She always said she just wanted someone who really loved her and couldn't find that fellow. Her life crumbled when she met Shaun and he took over her existence. That was five years ago. Alicia started snorting cocaine, and nothing else seemed to matter to her. Shaun was her supplier, and they partied all the time. Alicia lost her job, and soon after that Shaun went to jail for trafficking. That is when Alicia started selling to support her own habit, and the boys care took a back seat to her pursuance of "the love of her life – cocaine".

I watched my daughter change from a responsible adult to an irresponsible addict. I showed up at the house often to see that the boys were alright. I was a sucker for her stories, she needed $20.00 to get milk, or she needed help to cover the rent. The power got cut off in the winter and the boys couldn't stay in a cold house, so I paid the bill. I took the boys home with me and phoned social services. I was told that as a grandparent I had no rights, lots of mothers used cocaine or smoked pot, and occasional use was not reason to take children away from a parent. If a teacher or other professional person doubted that they were being taken care of, or if the police had reason to take the children, social services would step in.

Darren was just a child, and he took care of the household, took care of his brother and his mother. I know he hid facts from me to keep his mom from getting into trouble, but I couldn't keep turning my head when the grow op appeared in the house. I had cause to worry for the boys' health before the grow op, but now I had something to get my daughter charged with. I don't know if anyone can imagine the guilt I carried for that year, and the worry about almost everything that could happen to a drug addicted daughter and two young grandsons. What if the house caught fire, what if one of those questionable characters who came to the house for dope molested them, what if someone else threatened their mother for money she owed? And then I carried the guilt of squealing on her.

The night they arrested Alicia, they brought the boys to me and said they would be back in the morning to question them. I talked to the boys first to explain. Bradley had never seen the plants, had never been in the family room, but Darren had. We talked about this, and Darren said he would tell the police about the room when they came. I heard him crying at about 6 a.m. and went in to comfort him. He had wet the bed, something he had not done since he was three. He was sobbing, and as I held him, he said, "I'm sorry Grandma, but I just cannot do this to Mommy." I understood this, and so did the police.

As a first-time offender, Alicia was given a warning. But she had lost her car; the home was boarded up pending renovation and removal of marijuana plants and the most serious of all - she had lost her children. I took the boys to counselling. Alicia took to the street.

As Bradley said, we had not seen much of Alicia in the last four years. She would call occasionally to talk to her sons, and she was always invited to come to my house to visit them, there was a standing invitation for Sunday dinner. She rarely showed, and when she did, we had strained conversations. I would tell her all about her boys' lives, but it was hard for her to swallow the fact that I knew all about them, and she no longer knew them at all. It just hurt us both too much, so we started to talk about the weather. The fact that she came at all was due to Matthew. I am thankful for the support he gave to her; I have never really understood the compassion he had for Alicia, but he did take care of her these last years." (*I didn't want to say anything about Alicia's unhappiness in Matthew's care. She was after all paranoid all the time. He seemed like such a decent sort that I didn't pay much attention to her stories of how he was a control freak, wouldn't give her any money but bought cigarettes, clothing, and make-up for her, watched her like a hawk, and didn't trust her to be alone. She had told me that he was a sexual deviate, and she was his sex slave. How do you think he knows so much about the streets; she had asked me? Matthew had taken her party clothes and her red spiked heels away from her. She seemed to be afraid of him, and he seemed to covet the ground she walked on. I could never understand the relationship, but I was happy that Matthew kept Alicia off the street, fed and clothed her, brought her to visit her sons. She wasn't happy but she was safe, I thought. When she was healed and got her confidence back, she could start again, I told her I would help her when she was ready.*)

I have said many prayers, begged and demanded help, prayed for a miracle. I can't say the prayers have been answered. I had lost my daughter a long time ago, but I did not expect her to ever lose us. We were waiting for her to return to a normal life someday, perhaps she will when she has put in her time as an angel, as Bradley says, perhaps she will return at a higher value. But who could be of more value than a daughter, than a mother?

I cannot talk about the day I went to claim my daughter, how difficult it was to identify her, the day I had to admit that I could no longer help her, no longer wait for her to return to us. All I can say is that I will take the best possible care of the two sons she loved dearly. She could not find the way back to care for them herself."

Matthew: "I met Alicia two years ago when I was cruising the streets of Burnaby looking for my brother. My brother had been straight for several years and was going through a tough relationship break-up and I thought he may have returned to the street. I had invested so much in his healing, and I didn't want him to go back to drugs. I didn't find him, but I did find Alicia. I thought "my God, she is the most beautiful lady in the world". She was leaning on a streetlamp trying to keep herself upright and talking to the sky. I asked her to get into my Van and took her home with me. I knew I had to save her and had gone through all the steps of controlling an addiction before with my brother. She said she wanted to get clean and sober, she had gone into treatment centres a couple of times, but the local programs were too short and didn't solve the problem. They were just temporary dry up centres. At one rehab center she wrote a good-bye letter to the love of her life and let me read it. The love of her life was cocaine.

She would be fine for a couple of months and then she would disappear. Once the police phoned and asked me to pick her up at the station. Sometimes I would find her at a crack house, or on the street. I knew all her old haunts. I know suppliers, I know users, and I have my sources of information. Alicia took my Van a couple of times. I was always able to find her, and she always fought and cried, and I had to force her to come home so I could take care of her. Once I found her in an abandoned car shivering with cold. She had nothing but garbage bags to keep warm, so she had wrapped herself in them and early in the morning the condensation from her body in the plastic was making her colder than it was outside. She was street smart in some ways, but so innocent in others. She had been beaten by a couple of johns who had picked her up and left her in an alley. She had been pushed out of a crack house because she was too rowdy. My worst scare was when the police phoned and asked me to come to a shed behind an old packing house. Since Alicia was "known to police" they had my cell phone number to call if she was ever in trouble. She was crouched in a corner and there was blood down her legs, she was like a zombie. I carried her to the van and took her home, I was afraid of what might have happened. She did not want to go to the hospital. The truth was that she had just got her period and had no supplies; she had no idea that I thought she had been raped and injured. I held her for hours, and smoothed her hair, and told her how beautiful she was and how I would take care of her. She never ever said she loved me, but I thought she might one day after she was clean for awhile.

During her stay with me, Alicia smashed a clock because she thought there was a hidden camera in it, burned all my CDs in a garbage can because there were subliminal messages in them, and dug up a huge hole in the flower garden because she thought there was a child buried there. Her mind was being affected by the drug abuse.

The last six months, things were looking up. She had been clean and sober and was starting to go for walks. Until then she sat in front of the television all day, answering the voices who were talking in her head. She still talked to the voices, but I thought soon I would get her psychiatric help for her paranoia and schizophrenia. She promised me she would go to a rehab centre again, and we were doing research on some. She wanted to be able to get her own place, talked of getting her boys back, talked of getting her own financing, but a lot of the plans she was making made no sense at all.

On Friday, she had a long bubble bath, and put on clean jeans and make up and said she would be going for a walk and did not want me to go with her. She wore her new running shoes and carried her bag.

I started to worry when she didn't return for hours and drove around until the early hours to look for her. And you all know the rest."

Elizabeth (after the memorial): The day after her death Matthew drove us to the road where Alicia was found. The police report said a female, scantily dressed, was beaten to death, and thrown from the passenger door of a moving vehicle. There were no witnesses. It was Darren who noticed the red spiked heel at the side of the road and shouted, "Stop the car. That is Mommy's shoe!" the shoe he had seen her in at the bus stop years ago. I said to Matthew, "Did you not say she left for her walk in runners?" "Yes," he said, "she must have changed to her hooker clothes after she left." I nodded and made a mental note that I had one more phone call to make and this one would be easier.

And so, the small group of the people who loved Alicia talked on, trying to reconcile their own guilt and weaknesses, and share their loss. And as Matthew left my house, I looked out to see police walking around his van, waiting for him. I thought that things are not always the way they look. And I said to an invisible angel "*I am so sorry Alicia, I heard but I was not listening.*"

BASHFUL BRIAN

I have been fascinated with shoes on the road since I was 10. Fascinated or haunted by them, scared to death of them, they bring up memories – nightmares really. I feel that I must tell this story, perhaps it will erase the memory, perhaps it will allow me to forget, and maybe I could even forgive (*not Goddamn likely*).

My name is Brian. I can remember my mom coming home from her shift at Ed's 24-HOUR CAFÉ on Sunday when I was watching Walt Disney. My Mom did shift work, so I was home alone a lot. She looked so tired – her red hair done up in a bun with two little strands that had gotten loose from where she parked her pen above her ear. Her eyebrows were tight causing two little furrows between her green eyes. Tired, and lonely, she had no one at home but me. "I suppose you are hungry," she would say. Of course, I was hungry; I had made a bologna sandwich at noon – two pieces of nummy bologna with mustard and lots of butter between two pieces of "day old" bread. I don't think "day old" meant it was made yesterday – no I'm sure it wasn't! I was tired also, well bored, and lonely. I guess we shared loneliness.

When Belinda lived in the basement I wasn't alone so much. She was a day care worker and was home most evenings and weekends and she would spend some time with me. I loved Belinda. In winter, I would hide behind the fence when I knew she was coming home from work. When she got to the gate, I would throw a snowball at her and run. She would chase me around the yard and call me a little brat. When she caught me, she often said, "I don't have a date for supper, how about joining me for Taco's" and I would visit her in the basement. Belinda didn't have TV because she was saving up for a rainy day. We would play Monopoly or Scrabble or something after supper and listen to her country and western tapes. Many of the songs were sad, and many of them sounded lonely. Belinda liked "Make the World go Away" by Eddie Arnold. She would always tell me to listen carefully to the words of country songs, they told stories but some of them were just funny to me. We giggled a lot. Belinda would throw back her long black hair and laugh out loud. She had luscious big boobs that bobbed up and down when she laughed. When she hugged me, I would snuggle right into them and wonder how they could be so warming, so comforting.

Belinda and I were great friends, but she got married and moved to Vancouver with her husband. I really missed Belinda; things weren't the same without her. She told me she would be coming to visit her friends from time to time and would call me – perhaps we could go to a hockey game sometimes she said.

When my mom gave me a hug on her way to work, I would put my arms around her thin body and wish she wasn't so worn out so she could have soft mushy boobs like Belinda.

We needed the rent from the basement suite to get along, so Mom advertised in the Kamloops news for another renter. That is how Frank came into our lives. He seemed old to me, but Mom said he was younger than she was, and I think Mom had a thing for him. When he first moved in, she was giddy and silly. She invited him to supper on Sunday; I was happy about that because we had pork chops and mashed potatoes and apple sauce. And ice cream. That is how I knew she had a thing for him because we could never afford dessert. She said it was from her tip money, so she splurged. Those were nice times, because Mommy seemed happy, she would laugh and flirt with Frank and the furrows disappeared from the bridge of her nose. I had never seen my mom with a man – my dad had never ever seen me, don't know who he was or where he was, all that my mom said was "of course you had a father, do you think you were an immaculate birth?"

But things cooled down as the weeks went by – I don't think Frank was very interested in Mom. He had asked me several times if I wanted to come downstairs to watch TV with him. I enjoyed doing that because Frank always had chips or Cracker Jacks in bowls on the coffee table. He even sometimes asked me if I wanted a Coke, and I loved Coke. We would watch Little House on the Prairie or Bonanza; I loved Hoss and Little Joe and Adam and wished that I could visit a ranch with horses. There were lots of ranches around Kamloops. I said I would like to have a horse for my friend. I didn't have many friends – I was shy. The teacher called me "Bashful Brian" when Mom went to meet her. She asked Mom if there weren't other boys on our street that I could play with instead of just going home after school to watch TV.

One day when I went to the basement to see Frank, he had a picture of a boy a little older than me on the table. "Who is this," I asked, "is this your boy?" "He was," Frank said "but he got too big for his britches. You look like him, don't you?" I guess we sort of did look alike, we were both blonde and slim, wore blue jeans and runners. I thought he was cute and wondered if that meant that I was cute.

That evening we were sitting on the chesterfield, and Frank said, "Slide over here by me Brian, we look like bookends on each side of the sofa." I slid over some and so did he. After a while he put his hand on my leg. I just looked at it, it was old looking and hairy. He had black hair peeking out of his denim sleeve, kind of gross. I looked up at his face to see that he was looking at me too. His chin was rough from shaving, his nostrils had black hair in them too, he was looking at me kind of weird, but his eyes were dark brown and soft looking, kind looking. "I really miss that boy" he said, "we were good friends, and you make me think of him with your blonde hair and blue eyes. You are just as sweet as he was!" And Frank put his arm over my shoulder, and we just sat that way. I thought, this is ok, he is sad because he misses his friend, and we are friends, so this is ok.

In the spring Frank asked me if I would like to have a bike. Of course, I would rather have had a horse, but a bike would be good, most of the boys rode bikes to school. He said someone at work had a bike they were trying to sell cheaply and if I was a good boy, he would get it for me. I was always a good boy, but I would have to ask Mom if that was ok. Mom wasn't too happy about accepting it because we didn't need charity. But Frank talked her into letting me have it. When he brought it home, he helped me learn to ride it, and before long I was biking up and down the street going through the puddles in the street and feeling the wind in my hair. Mom was working late that night, so Frank asked if I would like to have a hot dog with him for supper. We sat on the back doorstep to eat because my jeans were all splashed and dirty. Frank said I should take off my dirty jeans and have a bath before Mom came home and I agreed. So, I went upstairs and poured my bath and climbed in. I had boats on the edge of the tub to play with, and I was sitting there playing with them when Frank came in. "You should be washing before you play cause the water will get cold," he said and grabbed the soap. He had never just come into our place before without knocking and Mom letting him in, so I was surprised that he would do this. "I can wash myself, thank you, and Mom says I should never let anyone in." I said, grabbing for the soap. Frank said things about me not being grateful for the bike and not trusting a friend and stuff and proceeded to soap my back saying that if my father were here, he would be helping me in the bath. I didn't know if that was true or not. Frank washed me all over, I mean my private parts and all, and he was breathing funny when he was doing that. Then he said he was sorry he couldn't stay to dry me and rushed back downstairs. I was glad that he was gone and got out of that tub and locked the door. I decided not to tell Mom that Frank had come upstairs.

Springtime with a bicycle made me spend a lot more time outside. Frank had a camera and started hanging out in the front yard when I was out and taking my picture riding my bike and stuff. He started giving me little presents, like a bag of marbles, or a game of jacks. A boy my age had moved onto our street and finally I had a real friend, he would hop on my bike seat, and we would double and go to the park. Tommy loved baseball, so we would play catch there until it was time to go home. Time for Tommy to go home, I really didn't have a "time to go home" most days. That was a fun springtime.

Except for one thing, Frank started to bother me. After all these years I still cannot accept the things that happened, or why I didn't tell my mom or my teacher or Tommy. No, I couldn't tell Tommy because he was my first real friend, and I didn't want him to not like me. How could I tell Tommy that when I was downstairs on Frank's couch, Frank suggested we play a little game? He unzipped his pants and told me there was something in there for me – could I find it. I reached into his pants and groped around a bit to see if there was a present there. His penis got big and hard, and he told me to touch it. "You've got to help me with this!" he said," put your hand around it and rub it for me" he said as he breathed into my ear and started nuzzling into my neck and shoulder. I tried to pull away, I wanted to run, but he said that as his friend I had to help him, and he undid the button on his pants and pulled his cock out of his drawers. You'll like this a lot when you see what we can do he said. The thing was big and ugly, I thought, and looked away. Frank covered my hand and started moving it up and down on himself, and breathing like a sick person, and holding me there with the other hand so I couldn't get away. I had to think of something, put my mind somewhere else so I started to think of Belinda's favorite song. *"Make the world go away and get it off my shoulders. Say the things you used to say and make the world go away."* That first time he didn't ask me to put my mouth on his cock – not that first time.

Summer holidays, Whoopee! I loved summer holidays, I had finished grade five and could play with Tommy every day, I was thinking. But Tommy went to stay with his grandma for all of July, what a bummer. I still loved horses, I had read Black Beauty and Misty and Phantom Stallion and any other horse story in the school library. Frank asked Mom if he could take me to his brother's ranch to pet the horses, and maybe I could ride one all by myself. We would go on Saturday and sleep over at the ranch in the Nicola Valley. His brother had a couple of kids my age and it would be fun. Mom said yes, and except for the fact that I had never stayed over anywhere but at Tommy's house, I was excited.

Frank had his car trunk loaded down with camping stuff, he said he might sleep in the tent, and I could sleep in the bunkhouse with the cowboys at the ranch. All I took was an overnight bag that my mother packed: toothbrush and paste, a hairbrush, some cookies, a clean shirt and underwear, and a calendar from Ed's 24-Hour Café that I was to give Frank's sister-in-law.

Not having been out of Kamloops before except for when we took the Greyhound to Penticton one summer to visit an aunt and swim in the lake, I didn't know where the Nicola Valley was or anything. After about five hours driving, we were entering the mountains, and I saw a sign that said "Jasper". We drove into a campsite, and Frank said he changed his mind, we would stay in Jasper and see the bears and elk and other wild animals, and go to the ranch on Sunday, this was a little side trip. As we were setting up the tent, Frank told the couple next to us that I was his nephew, and we were on a little holiday. I asked him why he lied, and he mumbled something, and said what fun I would have with the horses tomorrow.

We drove on; I read the signs: Yellowhead Hwy., Hinton, number of miles to Edmonton. I started to get really scared, he was kidnapping me, and Mom wouldn't even be worried yet. Sunday night we went off the main highway and stayed at some little campground. I was glad that Frank had brought two sleeping bags; I wouldn't have to "comfort him" as he put it. There was hardly anyone at this campground, but even at that he told me not to talk to any strangers (that wasn't likely to happen as I hardly talked to the people I knew) and just go straight to the toilet and back. He said we would head home tomorrow. That didn't happen.

When we stopped for gas Frank locked the car doors, I knew that I could still get out so what was the point? He bought sandwiches and we ate in the car or at the tent site. When I needed to pee at a gas station, Frank went with me, a hand gently on my shoulder, guiding me. I thought I could sneak to a phone, but I didn't have a quarter, heck I didn't have any money. Now Mom would be getting worried, we had been gone for four days. I started to plot how I could get away. Frank always talked nicely to me; look at those cows, that nice farmyard, etc. He made jokes about the farmers driving on the road and made small talk as we drove along. We were just on a little camping trip, my mother wouldn't mind, he said, and lied that we would phone her soon. We were on gravel roads; I didn't know any of the towns, maybe I would start shouting at the next service station, yell something to get attention. I went to the back seat to have a nap. We drove through a town called Meadow Lake, and I knew what to do. My name was in my runner, Brian B it said, so I took the calendar from Ed's 24-Hour Café and put it in the side of my runner and tucked it inside my pant leg. We stopped at a grocery store and went inside for some bologna and cheese and crackers. As I passed one of the counters, I quickly grabbed a pencil and put it in my pocket. I thought I would write "Help Me Brian B" on the calendar and leave the calendar in the store or give it to someone. There was no one in the store but the man who worked there, as soon as I put the pencil in my pocket he came towards me, he was a huge man with yellow teeth. "Got what you need there son?" he asked very gruffly, and I thought he saw me steal the pencil and got really scared. Frank bought a lot of groceries, and the man said "Not from around here are ya? Well, have a nice day."

Frank had parked alongside the road, passenger door to the ditch. As we got to the car, I stepped out of my runner and pushed the calendar into it and left it on the side of the road, then got into the car. There was no time to write the note. But now the police will find the runner, look at the calendar, and they would know there was a boy stolen from Kamloops, because Mom would have reported it. She might even know Frank's license plate, and they would chase up the road and stop the car and save me. We drove across the road to the service station, and I watched as my runner lay on the side of the road. Frank got out and checked the oil, and then he went and got oil and was putting it in, so I had a lot of time to watch. Three native boys came up to the runner, one of them took the calendar out and threw it in the ditch, and then he threw the runner to his friend and yelled "Catch this, chief." The three of them ran up the road, tossing the runner and yelling and laughing. Then Frank got into the car, and we drove away.

Next stop was just to check the oil again, and Frank discovered I only had one shoe. It was at the store wasn't it, he said, and what did that man say to you? He asked you if you had what you needed didn't he! He got very angry, and then he searched me and found the pencil. He said he wouldn't be able to trust me again if I was a thief. I could stop being a conniving little brat, didn't I appreciate that we were on a nice little camping trip? I knew we were in Saskatchewan; I knew there were mosquitoes, and I knew my mom would have gone to the police for sure. There were nice washrooms at the next service station. As per usual, Frank accompanied me to the bathroom. I sat inside the cubicle doing number 2 and knew what to do. I reached into the bowl and picked up a turd. It was kind of hard from all that cheese we ate. With it I wrote "Help Me, Brian B" on the wall. It got kind of messy at the end of Brian, but I could read it. I got another turd and smeared "from BC" underneath it, by then I could see Frank's shoes standing outside and I rinsed my hand in the bowl, wiped my hand with toilet paper, and flushed the toilet.

We ended the trip at a farmhouse, there were no others around. It was old and run down, there was no glass in the windows of the house, and there was a barn and a shed. Frank said it was his father's farm, and he had grown up here. He said we wouldn't be bothered here. We put the sleeping bags on the floor, but for the first time since we had left home, Frank grabbed my hand and pulled me down on the sleeping bag beside him, he kissed me on the mouth and told me what a sweet boy I was. He took off his clothes, and then took mine off. He put his hand on the cheeks of my bum and pulled me towards him. I brought the song back to my mind, *"Make the world go away and get it off my shoulder. Say the things you used to say and make the world go away. .... Make the world go away, Make the world go away."*

Over the next week, I tried to devise a plan of escape. We had campfires, could I send smoke signals, what if I started the barn on fire, what if I just ran down the road until I found a farmhouse or something. I would run away when we went to get groceries, I would yell and scream at the store. The days ran into the nights. *"Make the world go away and get it off my shoulder. Do you remember when you loved me before the world took me astray? If you do, then forgive me and make the world go away. Make the world go away."*

It was very early in the morning; I didn't know what day it was anymore because it didn't matter. I heard a car driving up the lane. I thought I would sneak out, but Frank was up and at the door before me. There were two cars; they had their lights on but no sirens. They came up fast and parked one on each end of the house. Four uniformed men stepped out of the cars, hands on their gun hip. Frank just walked out to them, just walked out like he was expecting company. He just walked out like nothing was wrong. They cuffed him and put him in one car. I got to ride in the other.

"Are you ok?" asked one police officer. "I guess, but how did you find me?" I asked. "Well, it was a storekeeper in Meadow Lake who put it together. He also picked up your shoe on the side of the road; hope you still have the left one."

CINDERELLA'S PRINCE

...behind every shoe on the road
there is a story, this is one of them

The neighbors were talking, a lesbian couple had moved into the vacant house on the corner of Greenlea Court. It was a beautiful lot surrounded by maple trees, with a very cozy little white house that had a wraparound balcony. The old couple that owned it had moved into a retirement community where there was no yard work, and the house had only been up for rent for a few weeks. Mrs. Smith had seen the ladies before the moving trucks arrived. They had stood looking at the house, and then one of them began to cry and the other put her arms around her and hugged her, damn lesbians. This used to be a respectable neighborhood. Most of the families had been here for years, raised their children, and were now retired. Mrs. Jones had seen them at the mailbox, sure enough; they had their arms around each other – hugging at the mailbox in full daylight. What were they going to tell their grandchildren when they asked about the ladies in the white house? This would have to be discussed.

Joanne and Sharon met at Dunbar& Dunbar, a chartered accountant firm. Joanne was one of the accountants there, and Sharon had been hired to create the firm's website. The two of them worked together on the project and got along so well that they became friends. Sharon was a dark-haired beauty with big brown eyes and eyelashes that fluttered when she talked. She was very creative and loved her work. Joanne was a bottle blonde, a very fashionable dresser (way out of the accounting league) and extremely intelligent. Her practical nature showed up in her accounting opinions and reflected in what she wanted on their website. The members of the firm could hear the ladies laughing and chatting as they worked together, and they commented on what a good team the ladies made. They were not at all surprised to hear Joanne ask Sharon if she would like to go for supper on the day they finished the website.

Joanne had grown up in Toronto, her parents were double income professionals, so it was expected that she would attend University after graduating from high school. She would get her degree and become independent before anything else. Because she was good-looking and intelligent, she had many, many offers to attend university functions, concerts, games etc. The bonus was that she also had a great personality, so any man lucky enough to get a date with her always came back for seconds. Joanne's parents were both Harvard Graduates, and they had told her for years that these would be the best years of her life. Until graduation she would have her nose to the grindstone, and once she got her career established there would be PLENTY of time to get serious, settle down, and have a family. Joanne lived at home while she attended the University of Toronto and lived it up! Her parents were rarely home, between working and traveling the world, so at times they were roommates, the rest of the time she was alone in the house.

In her senior year, she had met Danny at a homecoming party. Danny was infatuated with Joanne, and he wanted to possess this lovely lady. She liked Danny, and everyone said they looked good together. Danny was an average looking guy, but the way he carried himself demanded attention. He had charisma, and it wasn't long before Joanne found herself in love with him. Danny put the rush on her at her Graduation Ceremony. Danny was very charming, very romantic, and ready to settle down. Joanne's parents loved him and were pleased that their daughter may become the wife of an architect. Joanne admitted that she loved Danny, but there was a slight reserve that often nagged at her, something she couldn't put her finger on. She thought it must be that she had wanted to get her career underway before she got serious before she started thinking about marriage. But, she agreed to move in with Danny.

Joanne would be working at Dunbar & Dunbar as a junior and wanted to continue taking specialized accounting courses and become a Chartered Accountant. Danny wanted to get married right away, but Joanne had a funny gut feeling that she didn't understand, a kind of mistrust that could not be defined, so she would continue to put the decision off.

Before Joanne moved into his condo, she and Danny would use her grad gift from her parents, two weeks in Maui at a beautiful exclusive resort. They were having a wonderful time, until the night they went to the nightclub. Joanne felt like dancing, and Danny as usual did not. They shared a table with two other couples, and one of the gents asked if Joanne would like to dance. His wife was pregnant, and her feet were swollen, and she said, please dance with my husband for me! Joanne did so, and they danced several dances before sitting down with the group again. Danny was sullen, and he suggested they go home. "He is jealous," thought Joanne, "I have never seen this side of him before!"

Danny tried to pick a fight on the way back to their suite, but Joanne didn't want to argue. Before they went to bed, Danny poured two glasses of wine, and they stood out on the lanai and listened to the ocean. It was so peaceful and so calming to listen to the tide come in and wash out again. Danny wasn't calmed; he pushed Joanne up against the wall and pressured her to say that she wished he were more of a dancer. Joanne told him not to be so juvenile and went to bed. "I made him jealous," thought Joanne, "I will not be so willing to dance with someone else if it makes the man I love feel like this."

Danny surprised everyone with a proposal on bended knee in front of the entire family and the Christmas tree. Joanne said, "Yes, I do want to marry you."

On a sunny Saturday in June, a limousine arrived at her parents' house to pick up the bride and her father. "I am here to pick up Cinderella," said the limo driver, "I understand that there is a handsome prince awaiting." Her father held her hand in the limo, and said, "Cinderella, you are off in space, a penny for your thoughts!"

"I think I am being silly," she answered, "but I feel like this is the wrong ride, that I should be somewhere else. Like I am on the wrong bus, but don't know where I am going."

"Well," said Joanne's father, "I think this is what is called 'cold feet', a very common symptom of the betrothed on the way to the church. I believe you are doing the right thing, my dear. Danny is a wonderful man. He is already established in his profession, so there is no problem with security. He has loved you from the day you met, he told me he wanted you to be his the first time I met him. And you love him, so why the concern?"

"I think you put your finger on it, Dad, Danny wants me to be his. He wants to possess me. I want to be 'us,' do you understand what I mean?"

"Here we are at the church, Joanne. What I understand is if you are his, he is yours, and that makes 'us.' So, are we in or out, did I get dressed up and spend 20 grand for nothing? That makes the term 'give your daughter away' a misnomer for sure. Take a deep breath dear and be thankful for this wonderful first day of the rest of your life." And he held the limo door for the daughter he was so proud of.

Six months later, Joanne stayed late at work; one of her customers had come in at the end of the day and told her he had some serious fiscal year end decisions to make and wanted her advice before he moved ahead. Danny phoned the office twice. No one answered at the switchboard because everyone had gone home. He tried Joanne's extension, no answer. Joanne and her client were in the boardroom. When she arrived at home, Danny had worked himself into a fury. He said he knew she wasn't at the office, so she must have been out with someone, out for drinks or at a motel perhaps. Joanne explained the situation, and he called her a liar. He grasped her arm and squeezed it, hard, I know you are up to something; you have been sneaking around on me, haven't you? Joanne said, no, she loved him and didn't even think of cheating. "Liar" Danny yelled, and then his right fist was thrust into her left eye. He hit her again, and again, on the ear, the cheekbone, the nose, and her shoulder. Joanne had fallen to the floor, she was shocked, she was crying, but careful not to scream, that might anger him further. Danny left the condo, slamming the door.

Joanne cleaned the blood off her face, she didn't think anything was broken, but her face was swelling rapidly. She calmly applied cold compresses, took aspirin, and cried herself to sleep. Danny came home in the middle of the night, and when in bed, gathered Joanne in his arms. He told her how sorry he was that he lost his temper, asked how she was, told her he loved her, and it would never happen again. Joanne apologized for being late, said she would call him or leave a message if it happened again. She was sorry that she had caused him to do this; she must be more considerate of him.

The next time he hit her it was because she got a phone message from a man who did not identify himself. The time after that she was beaten because Danny's friend told him what a "hottie" his wife was. The excuses were always weak, and Danny always apologized, and Joanne was always sorry she made him hit her.

The partners at Dunbar & Dunbar became concerned. Joanne had missed too much work, her redemption was that she always caught up, and always phoned in if she was "sick", and she was a great accountant. She hadn't taken the specialty courses she had planned on taking, and had stopped talking about completing her CA. She worked in her closed office too much and wasn't bonding with the other accountants; she sent e-mails to them instead of walking to their offices to discuss matters. She arrived early, shut the door, and left late.

Mitchell, in the office next to hers, was not fooled. He knew that there were purple bruises under the well-done make-up. He knew that neck scarves were not in style this year. The hair gently falling over one eye was not Joanne's new hairdo. He gently knocked on her door and asked to come in. Seated in the side chair in her office, he cleared his throat and approached the subject. "We need to discuss your health, Joanne, we need to discuss your survival!" She looked at him slightly shocked, not shocked because he knew what was up, but shocked that he approached her about it. How many days had she come to work feeling sorry for herself, and seeing the reaction in one of her co-workers' eyes, know that they knew, but felt comfortable that no one would ever say anything? Joanne's father knew what was going on and ignored it. Since he never discussed the problem, she thought for sure it was "her" fault. Danny wasn't cheating on her, he was a good provider, and they seemed so happy together. Why did she continue to provoke him?

Mitchell talked to her for over an hour, he understood that Joanne loved Danny, but he was very informed about battered wife syndrome.[*] He asked her to seek counseling; he told her that it was never her fault, never! She thanked Mitchell for the concern, and it was left at that.

The day that Joanne found out that she was pregnant, she was delighted. Danny was also extremely happy that they would be having a baby and phoned everyone to make the announcement. They went to Deerhurst Resort for the weekend to celebrate. Joanne thought this would make a difference. A baby! A baby would complete Danny's world, now he would be a happier man. Joanne had seen Danny with babies, and children. He was gentle, and funny, and really enjoyed them. He would make such a good father. For days the couple floated on air in the excitement.

---

[*]   See footnote on Battered Wife Syndrome at end of story

Things were good for the first trimester. They invited their neighbors over to play cards one night, and the other three enjoyed a few drinks. Joanne went to the kitchen to get another orange juice, and the neighbor's husband followed. He put his arm around Joanne, and was telling her how fortunate she and Danny were and confided that he and his wife had been trying to conceive for over a year and were considering a fertility clinic. And then Danny walked in. He didn't look happy, but the neighbor just stood there with his arm around Joanne like he would his sister.

Later, while they were cleaning up the dishes, Danny let his anger consume him. He accused Joanne of being a slut and threw her to the floor. He hit at her with both fists, and then hoisted up her skirt and raped her there on their kitchen floor. Joanne tried to fight him off, but he was much stronger than her and pinned her to the floor. She got up and tried to get to the bathroom. Danny threw her against the table, then grabbed her arm and shoved her against the kitchen door. Joanne was badly hurt this time; she grabbed her car keys and headed for the door. Danny shouted after her but did not follow. "You come back here," he shouted, "you really made me mad this time." Joanne could hardly drive, and the tears kept blurring her vision. She felt the wet between her legs and prayed. When she arrived at the hospital, she was quickly put into an examination room. The doctor who examined her asked her if she would like to file a complaint. She said no. She had left without her purse and had no identification. The admitting nurse had ignored this and told her she would be able to bring it in later. The doctor knew this, and said that she still had time to file the complaint when she brought in her ID. "Thank you," Joanne said, "I need time to think about it, I may do that."

Livsharan and Deepinder had also married for love. They had begged their way out of the traditional arranged marriages both sets of parents had wanted. They were of the same status, and love got its way. Livsharan was a beautiful young woman; she had long dark hair and big brown eyes. They tried to follow tradition as much as possible – but most of their friends were Canadians and the couple wanted them to be comfortable at the wedding as well. Livsharan was her father's fifth daughter, she was the twinkle in his eye, and according to the older sisters was spoiled beyond reason, and always got her way. She wore blue jeans, went to university, dated Deepinder without permission, and worked out of the family business. She got everything she wanted, including Deepinder.

Deepinder had taken a year of college but was not sure what he wanted to do for a career. He was a natural athlete and had been an asset to every team he was on. Because he was a team player, someone suggested that he join the army. Deepinder read everything he could on the army on the Internet and ended up signing on for three years. He liked the discipline and training, he would fight for Canada if he was needed, but meanwhile he would become a heavy-duty mechanic.

Livsharan was concerned that someday Deepinder would be deployed, but he enjoyed the service so much, and she was happy when he was happy. Livsharan, "Sharan" as she was known at work was a web site developer. She was able to work at home if she wished, or at the office, or in client's offices. The company that she worked for was international, and this fit right into Deepinder's career if he should travel with the army. She knew that she could not bear to be separated from him but would wait and see how he fit into the army's plans.

CFB Petawawa was their first base after Deepinder's basic training. Deepinder fit into this way of life very easily, and Livsharan was happy that they could stay near their families. They were still close enough to attend all family get togethers, and there were many, their extended families being very large.

Within a year, their baby boy was born. Deepinder was ecstatic, he had the life he wanted, a beautiful wife he loved and a son. His life was full. Deepinder was a doting father and loved Livsharan even more now that she had given him a son. He tended to Amar when he was at home, changing him, feeding him, and playing with him as much as he could. He knew his time with the baby might be interrupted with his military service, and he wanted his memory banks to be overflowing to sustain him when he was away with the army.

When baby Amar was six months old, his father was deployed to Afghanistan. Livsharan had a very large support group, and although she hated to be a day without her husband, knew that she could get through it.

Only in Afghanistan for 4 months, Deepinder was killed in crossfire. Livsharan and Amar moved back home to live with her parents in Ottawa. To help her get through the days, she asked for work out of the home to develop web sites.

———————————

Joanne left Danny after the beating that caused her to go to the hospital. She still loved him but knew that she could not change the stripes on the tiger. She would survive very well financially and hoped that she would heal mentally. She asked her employer for a transfer to Ottawa and got counseling to help her understand what had happened. Danny had begged her not to leave and cried that he could not live without her. It took all her strength not to buckle to his pleas, but she did not.

So that is how Joanne met Sharan (Livsharan) at work, and their friendship continued to grow. Sharan loved her family, but moving back to live with your parents is hard on any independent person. The friends had a great idea; they would rent a house and live together. Although they had very different backgrounds and upbringings, they were compatible and were looking forward to moving on with their lives. Sharan would work at home as much as possible so that a day care would not be necessary.

———————————

Standing in the yard of the home they had found to rent, Sharan told Joanne that Deepinder would have loved the maple trees and the yard. Her broken heart felt empty again as it often did, and she started to cry. Joanne felt so badly for her friend, she put her arms around her and comforted her. "I think Deepinder is here, Sharan, he is happy that Amar will be able to kick balls around in this beautiful yard." So, Sharan snuffed it up, as she often did, for Amar.

The ladies living on Greenlea Court, where Joanne and Sharan were renting, were having coffee, and discussing everyone else as per usual. Mrs. Smith had made conversation with Sharan in the yard one day. "You know the new neighbor ladies and not lesbians at all. They are very nice. I talked to the dark one, Sharan, and she has gone through very tough times, her husband was killed in Afghanistan leaving her with the wee one. A widow at such a young age. I don't know the story of the blonde one, I was hoping Sharan would volunteer some information, but she didn't."

On a Saturday afternoon, Joanne announced that it was Sharan's time to have a day to herself and packed up her SUV with diapers and bottles and went off to the park with Amar. She spent time walking the paths, and then sat on a bench to watch the squirrels. Focusing her camera on a little beast near her took her attention away from the stroller. She sensed movement beside her and turned in time to see the man grab the baby from the stroller and run to the parking area. Joanne jumped up and ran after him, but quickly lost ground. She started yelling for help, but the park was quiet this fall afternoon. She lost the man for a minute in the parking area, and then saw the van pull away. Being the quick thinker that she was, she memorized the license plate, and then yelled, "Does anyone have a cell phone?

Dial 911!" A gentleman was quick to run to her side with the phone in hand, already relating the incident and the location, then handing a shaking Joanne the phone. Joanne gave the license plate number and the color of the van; she was not sure on the type. The police told her to stay where she was, and someone would be there soon. True to their word, a police car was there in minutes and the policeman asked her to accompany him to the station. As they were pulling into the station, the radio came on and the voice announced that the man driving the van had been apprehended, and he and the child were being driven to the same station. Joanne ran to the policeman who was carrying the baby, and upon being passed the baby hugged him to her, so thankful that he was ok.

Then she looked up, and there was Danny, handcuffed and restrained. "You deceiving bitch," said Danny, "you told me that you had miscarried the baby. You lied to me. Officers, that baby is mine!"

"For God's sake, Danny, look at him," yelled Joanne back, "this baby is brown. He certainly is not yours."

Danny looked at little Amar, a cute little brown baby in a sweat suit, with one little running shoe on. He looked very sheepish, very restrained, and very harmless. "I screwed up again, didn't I", he said as they took him off for questioning. This time she would lay charges, yes; she was tougher now and had all her confidence back. One officer returned to get her statement and apologized. "I guess the little guy lost his shoe, it is probably where we took him out of the van," he said, "and I have ordered a tow truck to bring the van in."

The lost shoe was not a big deal to Joanne. She had lost the baby she was carrying, she had lost her husband, and she had lost her Cinderella dream to the Prince of the Punch. "It can be replaced," she said, "the shoe is one thing that can be replaced."

Battered Wives Syndrome: as copied from: www.ccmentalhealth.org

Understanding the Syndrome, It was just a slap. He apologized and said he'd never do it again. But he did do it again and the next time he hurt her. He was contrite. She was confused. In the years after the first slap, the violence escalated. She was hospitalized twice. But she didn't leave. She loved him. He said he loved her. And he was always so sorry afterwards. It's important to understand why she stayed and what she can do to break the cycle of battering.

Mixed Messages Of Love And Violence Most of us have a need to see only the good in people, especially the people we love. When the 'love' signal is mixed with the "violence' signal, it's very difficult to see the violence for what it is. This is especially true if the violence has gone on for long periods of time, or if there is a long period between violent episodes.

Guilt And Blame Set In We understand that, for every effect, there is a cause. Battered women often feel, or are made to feel, that they are to blame for their battering. It is very difficult for them to place the responsibility where it belongs-on the batterer. Some people have said that a battered woman is very much like a prisoner of war because she is often dependent on her batterer emotionally and physically.

Poor Self-Esteem Reinforced A batterer is often verbally as well as physically abusive. He may tell his victim that she is worthless and that he is the only one who will ever love her. At the same time, he tells her that she doesn't deserve his love. The batterer might also try to isolate his victim from the friendship of others, from participating in social activities or from holding a job. He wants total control. And one way he gets it is by beating down his victim's sense of self.

Economics Play A Role Many women feel that they would not be able to make it on their own if they left the batterer, or if the batterer were jailed. A woman may worry that, without a mate, she won't be able to support herself or her children. These are very real concerns and must be addressed by any intervention.

Leaving The Batterer A battered woman needs to talk to people who can help. Friends and relatives can be supportive and helpful, sometimes providing emotional stamina, which the victim does not have, for herself. Community service agencies, especially battered women's shelters, and women's advocacy groups, can help the battered woman leave her battering relationship and turn her life and the lives of her children around.

BERTHA'S BUNIONS

...behind every shoe on the road there is a story, this is one of them

It was cold and damp this morning, and consequently Bertha had a great deal of trouble getting out of bed. She was not sure if it was the sciatica again, or just a back problem, but she had to hold onto the bed stand and try to swing her legs to the floor. Once she was standing, the pain shot up her right leg and it gave way as she stepped forward. Painfully she progressed to the shower, the hot water would feel good, and she would remember to hang onto the railing in case her leg gave out again. Because she lived alone, she could not afford to fall and miss work. After her shower, she walked around her house trailer a bit and the pain subsided gradually. She thought that if she had had a better life she would be retiring soon, but no use dreaming about it, she had to go to work.

Bertha greeted the other housekeepers at the Blue Bird Motel. Olive's life was much more complicated than Bertha's. Joe was a fall down drunk, and occasionally mean to Olive. Her two sons were bums, and always borrowing money from their mom to "feed the children" they would say. "Bring them over for supper" Olive would suggest, because she knew the cash might not hit the IGA. The other housekeeper, Yulia, was a sweet young girl from Bosnia, and she and her boyfriend were trying very hard to make enough money to live without asking for assistance. They lived very meagrely, he found odd jobs in town to help pay for their basement suite and she was now on full time at the Blue Bird. They never quite made it to payday and Bertha often gave Yulia a $20 to get her through to the next Friday. Truckers often left the housekeepers tips, especially if they had got drunk and puked on the carpet or something that required extra work. The ladies shared all tips and sometimes they even all went to the diner for pie and coffee on a break.

After loading her cart with fresh sheets and towels, Bertha made her way to Unit 101. Her bunions hurt so badly that tears came to her eyes, but she shuffled her way as fast as she could. The shoes that she had picked up at the Salvation Army Thrift shop were ill fitting, she would have to get time to check again and see if any wider toed oxfords were on the shelf in size 8 or larger, something that would give her less pain. Reaching Unit 101, she opened the door to look at her first cleaning job. Whoever stayed here last night was a pig, she thought. How could someone make such a mess in one night? She picked up McDonald's wrappers and the stench of the onions upset r thi᷈ ᴇarly in the morning. She picked up the beer bottles and ᴵs, not one of them had hit the trashcan. Cigarette butts in the ᴛay were soon taken out to the cart with the other garbage, and an attempt was made to freshen the room by leaving the door open and turning on the bathroom fan. "This asshole couldn't even piss straight" Bertha muttered. She tried to clean the burn mark left on the edge of the sink from a parked cigarette, washed the shaved whisker bits down the sink, cleaned the counter. Lifting the toilet seat, she attacked the bowl with a brush and Old Dutch. The shower and bathtub hadn't been used, not that this surprised her. After she had windexed the taps and mirrors, sprayed Lysol in the room, and mopped the floor, the bathroom looked usable again. The lino was very worn, but when it was clean, it was presentable. Back to the bedroom she went, she took her painful shoes off at the door and grabbed the Hoover. She had learned how to strip the bed without looking at the sheets years ago. Stuff you see on sheets could ruin your whole day, but once they were rolled and into the laundry bin on the cart, they were gone. She would have to check them at the laundry in case any spot remover was required, but that would be after lunch, and somehow things were more bearable after lunch. One day Bertha made an exercise of trying to figure out how many cups of bleach she had used in the lifetime. Could you fill a swimming pool with that much, or would you need a small lake? These days people were starting to talk about saving the environment, and "green" laundry products, what if they knew just how much bleach Bertha had personally put into the town wastewater! She guided the Hoover around in her stocking feet, they felt so much better unbound, and even though the carpet was worn, it looked good when freshly vacuumed. "Fresh as a daisy" she said as she locked Unit 101 up and started off for Unit 102.

She and Walter had stayed at a motel just like this one on their only holiday. Walter worked for the town sanitation department when she met him and worked for the town right up until the day that he died. They had a good life together, she and Walter. They married when they were 19 and had three beautiful daughters. They had had their heartbreaks all right. Their first trial was when she was 23; she had a very difficult pregnancy. Bertha was sick all the time and had trouble looking after her 2-year-old daughter Lizzy. Walter was such a help when he was home! He would rub her shoulders and her feet and kiss her tummy and ask it to get better and keep their baby safe, but it was not to be. The baby was born premature and was the scrawniest little thing Bertha had ever seen. His little chest was caved in, and he never did breathe on his own. They couldn't hold their son, but they could put a covered hand into the incubator and touch him a bit. Soon they were faced with burial costs and giving the baby a name. Walter wanted to name him Walter, but Bertha wanted to save that name for a healthy son, one that would take Walter's place in the world, so they named the baby after their fathers, good sturdy names for a namesake that was never strong or sturdy in hopes that he would be healthy in another world. Bertha left the hospital with the baby blankets and sleepers, after months of sickness and labour that had nothing to show for it. The heartbreak was unbearable. There never was a son named Walter, and Bertha always regretted that.

Walter insisted that Bertha stay at home and look after their girls, he wasn't much for wives having to go out and work and said he would look after the living if she would look after the life. Well, that was fine until the accident. Walter's brother had a farm just out of town, and Walter helped him with the seeding and harvesting as needed. One September Walter was helping with the combining. The tractor had been moody and as old machinery would be, needed a lot of TLC. Walter had been under the belly of the tractor tinkering with the rods when the tractor rolled back and over Walter's chest and legs. Walter dragged himself from under the old Massey and waited for his brother to notice that he wasn't bringing the tractor back to the field. Bertha got the call from the hospital on their party line and could hear the gasps on the line from the eavesdroppers when the doctor said "critical" situation. Walter was in the hospital for a long time. If the accident had happened when Walter was on the garbage truck, the town would have looked after them quite nicely, but it didn't happen on the job and Walter had limited coverage. The town looked after them for awhile, but Walter didn't get back to work for 2 years, and something had to be done to take care of living expenses and hospital costs. Bertha applied for work for the first time in her life. The girls were all in school, and they could make sandwiches, macaroni, and some other things. Bertha was hired at the meat packers. She was a strong woman and worked hard. The job required that she stand on her feet for 8 hours a day, and she never did have a good pair of shoes, she knew that was why she had the foot and back problems that she had today.

Well things are delivered in threes, so there was a third heartbreak in the lives of Bertha and Walter. Darlene started to feel sickly when she was twelve, first Bertha thought it was girl problems and treated her with aspirin and hot tea. But after awhile, Bertha took her to the doctor, and he ordered blood work. Darlene had leukemia, and there was no treatment, no cure. They let her try to live a normal life if she was strong enough, but there came a time when Bertha had to give notice and quit work for awhile to stay at home to look after Darlene. Walter had problems walking ever since the accident, and even though he worked full time, he couldn't take on a full workload, so never ever got a very good paycheck. The town felt sorry for him, so he would have a job for the rest of his life but didn't get any advancement. They would have a very hard time financially with Bertha not working, and medical costs for Darlene, but they would make it. When Darlene went to the hospital for the last time, and took her last breath, Bertha thought her heart would quit as well. "Lord, I have taken the challenges that you have given me this far," she told him, "But this one is too much to bear, I think I will cash it in now as well!" If it weren't for the love that Walter gave her, she would have died of heartbreak for sure. She went through the stages of blaming herself because she had to work, and blaming Walter, and blaming God, but eventually had to face Darlene's death as unavoidable, unexpected, unacceptable, and undoable. Life must go on.

Bertha was hired back at the meat packers and stood her own for many years knowing that someday she would no longer be able to stand for 8 hours at a time. She and Walter helped Lizzie with a few dollars when she got married. Lizzie married a truck driver, and although she was often lonely during his long treks, they had a good life and Bertha and Walter no longer had to worry about Lizzie turning out right. When she could no longer stand for a shift, she quit working at the packers and with luck on her side , she got a job at the motel. Then the worst thing that could happen to anyone happened to Bertha, her life was shaken by the death of her husband Walter.

The routine at the Blue Bird was basically the same everyday, but it depended upon how many units were rented the night before. If there weren't too many units to clean there were other jobs to do to fill in the time, mattresses had to be turned; the floors could be waxed and polished, windows could be cleaned. In the kitchen units, the fridges could be defrosted. There was always something that could be done to fill in time until noon. At noon all the units were always ready to rent again, and the ladies could have lunch. They had a small table and a little fridge in the laundry room, and here they caught up in each other's lives. "How is it going this month, Yulia" Bertha asked. It was the third week of the month, and this was usually a tight time for Yulia and her husband. "We still have some dry goods, and I still have a little cash for bread and milk, thank you for asking." Yulia said. "Could I spot you a $20.00 to get some meat?" asked Bertha, "you have to keep a little flesh on those bones when you work so hard, I can afford to lend it to you until payday." "I really hate to borrow, Bertha, but it would be very nice to make a big stew, or some soup, to hold us until I get paid. I was hoping we might get a nice tip this week, but I didn't get anything this week." "Neither did I, and you should have seen Unit 101 today. Pugh. Tipping just isn't thought much of in the prairies."

Olive joined the ladies, jubilant as she stepped in the laundry room, "Ladies we are rich. $15.00 in tips today. Well, a ten-dollar tip, and the rest in change under the cushion of the chair. Racy Lacy took a room last night, and that hooker always considers us working girls. I guess being a working girl herself; she knows how hard it is to make a buck. Maybe the three of us should consider working on our backs instead of on our feet." At this comment, the ladies all broke out in laughter, Yulia was skin and bones and looked more like a boy than a lady of the evening, Olive was rotund, and her face was pock-marked, Bertha's ankles were swollen wider than her shoes and she was old. None of them was well dressed, and it would take a heck of a lot to make them look like hookers. "Well, Bertha, my prayers are answered," said Yulia, "a fiver will get us some meat, and perhaps

I can start the month off with my whole paycheck instead of owing you some money this time, what are you ladies going to do with your five?" "Hide it from the old man" said Olive, "and hide it from my sons, I need some lady stuff at the drugstore, some nice lotion, and some deodorant, that's what I will do with mine!"

Bertha didn't know what she would do with hers right now because she was deep in thought. Every time Racy Lacy was known to have taken a room, it upset Bertha, because it made her think of her third daughter, Betsy. After Darlene died, Betsy was uncontrollable. She would go out at night when still in Junior High School, party all the time, run around with riffraff, and Bertha was always sure she would end up pregnant and they would be faced with that problem. Bertha blamed herself because she had to work since the girls were young, but Walter didn't blame the work, he said Betsy was just a bad seed, and he surely didn't want to put any blame on poor dead Darlene, she had no part of her sister turning wild. Betsy drank and smoked and got into all sorts of trouble, and then she ran away with some guy when she was in grade 10. She phoned collect once from Vancouver to see if they could wire her some money and told her parents that she was doing what ever there was to do to make a buck. Bertha was sure this meant she was a prostitute, or a thief. Because they didn't send any money, they didn't hear from her again and Bertha thought she might even be dead but had no way to find out. Lizzy would phone Bertha on all the special days, and when it was to say, "Happy Birthday", Bertha valued the call the most, because nobody else was celebrating this day, so it meant that Lizzy had remembered her mother on this day. One child out of four to get a birthday call from, Bertha would tear up and feel so guilty that she would get a pain in her abdomen, what did she do wrong to deserve this? And to lose her husband and to still keep on living, what was the use in going on?

"Buck up Bertha" Olive shouted, "you can't change what you can't change, you are thinking about the lost lamb again aren't you. Well, there is laundry to be done, and sidewalks to sweep, and garbage to get to the bin, and we need your help in here lady." So, they started unbundling the sheets, looking for and treating the stains, and getting the towels into the machines. Yulia came over and gave Bertha a bony hug; it is hard to stay depressed when you get a bony hug. "Would you mind giving me a lift to the drugstore, Bertha?" asked Olive, "I am thinking to spend this five today so that I don't have to lie and hide it from anyone, it will be gonzo." "Sure, if you don't mind riding in the beater!" Olive learned to drive their Chevy 15 years ago, and it still got her where she needed to go. That meant that Walter had been gone for 10 years, well the time had gone by fast. Bertha had borrowed more on their house trailer loan when Walter died, enough to pay for his funeral. She had chosen a modest coffin, and the town had given her a big cut on the burial plot since Walter had helped maintain the cemetery for years after he was transferred from the sanitation department. Bertha really wished that she could get a headstone for Walter, and for Darlene, and a little lamb or angel to stand over the grave of their baby boy. She would have to work until the loan was paid up, and then she figured she could live off her old age pension money. Things would be tight, but she was used to that and knew how to budget her money. No frills, no luxuries, cheap meats, coupon shopping, Thrift shop wardrobe, she had been practicing this for years, so her life wouldn't change one bit.

So, when the laundry was all folded, and sorted for the next day's labours, all three ladies got into the Chevy. They were tired, they were always tired after their shifts, but they were still cordial to each other. Bertha dropped Yulia off at the end of her block, nothing was very far away in a small town, and Yulia usually walked to and from work. Olive and Bertha continued to Main Street, and Bertha parked in front of the dollar store. The ladies both went into Samuel's Drug Store, and Olive started looking at the prices of lotions. Bertha looked around without really zoning in on anything, and then she walked up to the counter with Olive. Olive paid for her lotion and deodorant, and then Bertha reached her five out to the clerk, and said "I'll have a Quick Pick please, with the extra." "That's five dollars, thank you," said the clerk.

Bertha wasn't sure what came over her, she usually didn't waste money on Lottery tickets, but she didn't have to hold back money to lend Yulia this week, so it was either that or ice cream and pie, hard decision. Bertha always spent her tips on something special, even if that special was a little better soap, or Kleenex to use instead of blowing her nose on that cheap toilet paper that made her nose red, or real milk instead of powdered. She tucked the ticket into her purse, not smiling about it though, more like scolding herself for being so impulsive. She dropped Olive off at her yard, shaking her head at the used cars and junk that was collected there, and hoping the loudmouth didn't shout something obscene out the door to them for Olive coming home late.

Bertha waddled to her trailer, she should have bought bunion pads, she was thinking, or some more aspirin to take down the swelling. Well, what was done was done, she would just have some soup and put her feet up and pet her cat and the purring would lull her off to sleep and her feet wouldn't hurt until she turned over.

Tuesday morning dawned, same old, same old. Walk until you are more limber, shower; get to work, blah, blah, blah. Bunions killing you. Legs swelling up. Cleaning up after strangers. But then there was coffee break in the laundry room, and the ladies had a good chat and a few laughs. Bertha told Olive she sure smelled better this morning; she must have used her new pit stick. And Yulia told them how she had the stew meat in the crock pot, and it looked like her hubby was getting on permanently at the machine shop at the first of the month, and things were looking pretty good for them. They were looking forward to applying for their Canadian citizenship; heaven is here on earth she told the ladies.

Bertha was worried about the old Chevy, looked like she would need new tires when winter came. How would she budget for new tires? Well, she had a few months to get started on it, and she had friends who gave her vegetables in the fall, which really helped with the grocery money. Lizzie always did preserves and gave some to her mom. Bertha started thinking about what she would do if she had to quit work, for one thing what would she do to fill her time. She was too old to take on babysitting, and she couldn't stand to do much ironing or housekeeping. She maintained her little flower patch around the trailer, but that didn't take very long. She probably would die of boredom.

On Friday over lunch the ladies looked over the local newspaper that someone had left in a unit. "Local winner of Lotto 649" it said. Not the big one, 5 plus the bonus, shared by 4 people. That would be about $75,000.00. "Lucky stiff" said Olive, "hey Bertha, it could be you." "Well, wouldn't that be the cat's meow, "said Bertha.

And it was the cat's meow. She HAD the winning ticket. And as Bertha drove to the cemetery to tell Walter, and plan his headstone, she laughed out loud. Then she slipped off those horrible oxfords and threw them out one at a time -out the Chevy's window.

There is always a story behind those shoes found alongside the road!!

BANKERS' BROWN

As a journalist in Kelowna B.C., I was assigned to an interview with a successful local businessman who had retired and was now sitting on a board of directors of Alpha Technology Inc. The chapters below are quotes from the interview, his life as he saw it – then I will relate the story of his life as told by his family, friends, and acquaintances. Jennifer Jones: Kelowna Tribune.

CHAPTER ONE

Sarah went into labour around midnight, she didn't get excited – she had done this eight times before. She roused Ted and told him the babies were coming. He knew the routine: call his sister as she was a mid-wife, light the wood stove, put the water on to boil, and have a cigarette. Yes, he had done this many times before. He wondered whether he would get lucky this time, 7 girls and one boy so far (one still born which was also a girl). Sarah had only made one visit to the doctor and that is how she knew she was expecting twins. The first little one entered the world, a robust baby boy with a good set of lungs, minutes later the second entered – a scrawny boy but alive and kicking. Sarah didn't have names ready, but the other children (aged 5 to 15) helped, thus Edward and Albert (royal names for little kings) joined the family. The sisters coddled their new brothers and took turns taking care of them. Their older brother just looked at them and frowned, two more to share the meagre meals, and that little Eddie looked like he would have a good appetite.

Sarah took the babies in stride. Once a week she would take the bus to downtown Edmonton and shop for groceries. With the $25.00 Ted gave her from his wages she would somehow get enough food for 10 children and two adults. She asked the butcher if he had saved her any scraps and soup bones this week for her dogs. The grocer kept the outer lettuce leaves and whatever vegetables he could for Sarah's rabbits. She used what she could out of the lot for the family stews and actually did feed the rest to the pets. It helped when Ted was successful at hunting and brought home deer, moose, or pheasant. Ted was a fair provider, and they owned their two-story home with no indoor bath facilities or running water. Life was hard but it was good, enough money was always a problem, and when Sarah and Ted heard their children laughing and playing in the back yard, they were not sorry that they were good Catholic parents and hadn't practiced birth control.

CHAPTER TWO

The twins were in their second year at St. Joseph's school. Eddie was in second grade, but Albert was held back to repeat grade one as he was "immature". Eddie wasn't a great student but he liked to please his teacher so he tried to achieve all that he could. He loved to be outdoors kicking a ball, wrestling with his friends, racing, and climbing trees. Sarah "made" him wait for Albert after school so they could walk home together. Eddie loved walking home from school, rarely on the sidewalk, but rather around trees and through yards and petting dogs, and just "being a little brat" according to his sisters. Their older brother had already left home to join the army.

CHAPTER THREE

As the years went on the sisters left home one by one to get married or to join the army. Albert and Eddie were altar boys, and their parents saw to it that they went to church and were good Catholic boys. There were only three children left at home: Patricia who was five years older than Eddie and Albert, and the twins who were teenagers. Patricia hadn't been a healthy child and at the age of fourteen her rheumatoid arthritis was so advanced that she could no longer walk and was wheelchair bound. Sarah took it all in stride and gave Patricia as much care as she could. Albert was jealous of all the time and favors his mother gave to Patricia. Eddie befriended Patricia. He loved to push her wheelchair around the neighborhood and the fairgrounds. Their house backed the Edmonton Exhibition Grounds, and what they loved to do was go around and look at the horses at the racetrack and talk to the jockeys.

When Eddie was in high school, he was on the football team and became interested in girls. A typical teenager. He and his friends would have garage parties, with girls, playing rock and roll on their record player, good clean fun. Eddie took Patricia to some of them when she felt well enough. He was doing well at school, but still more interested in sports. One of his teachers told Sarah and Ted at a parent-teacher interview that Eddie would not have the grades to go to college, and should be looking at what trades he was interested in. That sparked something in Eddie, and he was quoted in the yearbook as wanting to become a chartered accountant. Well, math was one of his best subjects (second to science and Phys Ed.)

CHAPTER FOUR

Eddie was off to the Southern Alberta Institute of Technology in Calgary. That was a very large step for him. He left behind his loving parents (Albert was still living at home and having quit school after grade 10 was learning to be a mechanic at a local garage), the neighborhood that held his whole life's memories, his girlfriend, his friends, his beloved sister Patricia, and he moved out of his comfort zone. At SAIT Eddie loved the challenges of college. He studied electronics, but what he really liked was socializing, Eddie was a people-person. His roommate talked him into joining the student's union, and in his senior college year he was the president. Eddie became the guy to know on campus, he flirted with many of the girls, but he was true to his high school sweetheart.

Eddie had worked since he was twelve. He had a paper route. He had a job delivering hot fresh doughnuts from a popular little bakery in his neighborhood. In his high school years, he worked at a mattress factory, wrapping and preparing mattresses for shipping. He was an independent fellow. To go to college, he got a Queen Elizabeth Scholarship. He may not have become an accountant, but he did know how to budget, his parents had been life coaches on getting by with very little. In his graduating year he was "head hunted" by one of the most aggressive and growing companies in the sixties, a company called Xerox. Being a graduate of a technical school qualified him to be a photocopier technician, so Eddie was ready to start earning good wages.

CHAPTER FIVE

Eddie moved back to Edmonton – his territory of choice. In the first few years of working for Xerox, he bought a house, got married to his high school sweetheart , had a daughter and became a member of the Rotary Club. Following his achievement track record, Eddie became a very active member of the club and one of its leaders. He took his role of husband, and then father seriously. He had a lot of good friends, some from high school, some from work, and some from the club. He even helped Albert get a job as a technician. Now that was perfect for Albert who had very good mechanical skills.

One of Eddie's challenges was the fact that his job required him to be on the road most of the week, and his territory was large extending to Northwest Territories. He loved the work but found it lonely and being a people person sought some camaraderie in the local bars. Being a very good-looking young man with a great physique, and the requirement that he wear a suit on his jobsites made him a target for many young women, not to mention that he was a "sweet talker".

Eddie got tired of being on the road.

Eddie wanted to climb the ladder, he became team leader and after 10 years became a manager. He moved from Service Manager to Regional Manager, and to go any higher in the company he would have to take a position in Toronto at head office. He decided instead to start on an entrepreneurial journey. He had always been enterprising and very excited to become his own boss. Before long he had a successful business selling communication devices in Edmonton and had a staff of five. Hard work (and luck) led to success, and he set up businesses in every major city in Alberta.

His only vice was smoking. With a desk job he was now up to a package of Export A per day. One day at home he picked up his pack of cigarettes, put one in his mouth and went to find a light. No matches to be found anywhere, no lighter, he could try to light the cigarette on the electric stove burner, Eddie panicked. Here we see what a strong will Eddie had, he calmed his panic and threw the whole pack in the garbage – and never touched a cigarette thereafter.

At the office he settled into his swivel chair at his oak desk, signed cheques, made big money decisions, and life was good. He was still very active and played racquet ball at a club, played hockey on a businessmen's team, taught his daughters to ski, and coached their baseball teams, Eddie even gleaned a few trophies from competitive racquetball. He drove a Cadillac, had a Motor Home to take his family on holidays, moved to an elite district in the city. He and his family went to Hawaii on holidays. His hard work had paid off. He was independent, he was financially well off, he loved his role in life. Unfortunately, his first marriage broke down, they just outgrew each other.

He met the love of his life on a business venture and married a second time. Eddie bought a few more businesses, some very successful, some not so much. His role became that of a director. He still enjoyed the role of leading and directing, but found his family became the major joy in his life. The highlight of his life was his role as Grandpa. He was grateful for his extended family, and the loved ones that he had lost: his parents, his sisters, and his beloved Patricia – all of whom had major influences in his life, but the biggest influence of all were those little Grandkids.

He was ready to retire - to enjoy the good life. He would have all the time he wanted to golf (of course he was very good at that and had a low handicap and ran the senior men's league). He loved to cook and would have time to create some specialties. He would have time to give his grandchildren more of his wise words, to share his experience and wisdom even if they didn't ask for it. He had travelled the world, he had made many acquaintances, he loved and was loved, he was ready to have those golden years he had looked forward to.

EDDIE'S LIFE AS OTHERS SAW HIM IE. WHAT EDDIE DIDN'T TELL THE JOURNALIST.

RE: CHAPTER ONE

Lydia: Eddie's mother did house cleaning for my mother in Edmonton. When she became pregnant for the 8th time at the age of 45, she was devastated. She had 8 children to feed now on her meagre housekeeping pay and her husband Ted's truck driving wages. She wasn't sure if they could stretch the money any further, and the doctor had said she was carrying twins. And she would not be able to work in the last month or after for awhile. She was hoping they would be girls as girl's clothes could be passed down, but Ted really wanted boys to go hunting with him.

RE: CHAPTER TWO

Dolly: My first memory is of being in my mother's rocking chair holding my baby brother, Albert, singing and rocking him – I was 10 years old. He was a colicky baby and needed coddling most of the time. I think his twin Eddie hogged most of the milk from our mother's breast and Albert was just always hungry. When the boys were two, they were a real handful. I can remember Eddie taking toys away from Albert and making him cry. Eddie was a sneaky little brat even then. He would steal Albert's toast and say he hadn't taken it; he would hide toys that Albert liked so he could play with them later. Eddie was bigger and stronger than Albert right from birth, and Eddie had a personality that we all loved. I can't say that Mom favored either one of them, but I do remember when Albert got older, he was still demanding. He would ask Mom to butter his toast even when he was plenty old enough to do it himself and she would butter it for him.

The older sisters in the family were responsible for the little ones, and once in awhile we would resent it, but sometimes they did come in handy!! One of my older sisters was a bully. she would give money to Eddie and demand that he walk to the corner store to buy her cigarettes. If Eddie refused or snivelled about it, she would swat him and threaten him – so he would go. Most of us girls couldn't wait to grow up and leave home. I fell in love with a swooner. I would sneak out to dances to be with him and listen to him sing. When I was 16, he joined the army, married me and I went to live with his parents in Winnipeg. So, I really wasn't around when Eddie was a teenager.

RE: CHAPTER THREE

Albert: I remember when we were about seven Eddie started the rabbit hutch on fire. In those days we had a burning barrel in the back alley, and our father was the one who burned the garbage. We used to walk to school down the back alley, then across the railway tracks. One afternoon we were on our way home, and Eddie took matches out of his pocket, he was fooling around with the flames, and then he decided to light the burning barrel. When the fire started to flare up, it caught the side of the rabbit hutch and started it on fire. I ran into the house yelling, and the fire department was called. Our sister Patricia was really upset, she was twelve and she ran into the hutch to try to save some rabbits. The fire department scolded both, Eddie for lighting the hutch on fire and Patricia for going into a burning building. Eddie said he didn't know that dad pulled the burning barrel away from the hutch when he lit it, of course, he acted like he was innocent, he was always innocent.

Some of the things Eddie led me into were dangerous. We had lumber yard across the tracks, and Eddie would encourage me to go jump the lumber piles with him. I was scared to jump too far over the lumber, but I didn't want Eddie to think that I was. He would badger me and tell me that I was a chicken and so I would muster up the courage and climb with him – that is until the day that I missed the landing and fell to the ground in pain. Eddie wasn't very kind to me usually, but he did help me get home and when I was taken to the hospital, we found my arm was broken and it was put into a cast. Eddie didn't get into trouble because it was all my fault of course!

When we were teenagers, I really didn't hang out with Eddie and his buddies. I joined the Army Cadets and spent a lot of time in that group. I was never in the same grade as my twin, so we didn't have many buddies in common. I spied on Eddie and his friends a couple of times when they were having a garage party. Once I saw them all smoking and making fun of each other. They were drinking beer. Once I saw Eddie trying to kiss a girl and getting slapped in the face. I loved that!! So funny!! I was bullied at home by my older sister, and I was never comfortable around my twin. I guess I liked him, he was my twin, but we were never close. He was an athlete, the girls liked him, he liked hunting with Dad, and I didn't. It was always cold and damp and miserable sleeping in a tent and getting up early to kill a bird I didn't like to eat wasn't my idea of fun. I would rather go grocery shopping with Mom and help carry her groceries. We were po we bought the clearance items, the bananas were brown, we got Easter chocolate after Lent and Eddie says he never ever had an Easter bunny with ears. Well, neither did I but I always thought that Eddie bit the ears off all the bunnies just being selfish.

After I left school, I worked for Edmonton Ford. I still lived with our parents, so I was able to save money, and I bought a brand new 1962 white Ford Fairlane. It was the envy of the guys and Eddie being very popular was asked to be in parades and later in wedding parties. He would come to me and ask if the Fairlane could be used as his friend's wedding car. I would consent, wash my car, fill it with gas, help Eddie decorate it, and then he would inform me that I was not invited. I should have stood up to him, I should have said the deal is off, but I just sulked back into the house and grumbled.

RE: CHAPTER FOUR

Janey: Eddie and I met when we were in grade 10. We had some friends in common in the neighborhood and we were at a garage party. I was thrilled when he asked me to dance, and later we talked. We had a lot in common. Everyone said we looked good together and we started hanging out. When we graduated Eddie went to Calgary to go to SAIT and I stayed in Edmonton to go to U of A, so we only saw each other when Eddie could come home on a break. We were in love and going steady. The plan was to get married when Eddie graduated, I knew he would be true to me, and we had a wonderful life planned. We were good innocent teenagers. Years later I learned that he dated someone else in Calgary and was never honest about it. Eddie denied that of course.

RE: CHAPTER FIVE

Rick: Eddie and I worked together at Xerox and I learned a lot from him. He taught me the technical side of the business, but mostly he taught me monkey business. We travelled out of town together and believe me we had a girl in every town. The company wanted us to share motel rooms, but we refused to do that because it would cramp our action when we brought broads back to our room. After work we always went to the bar for a scotch or two, and then we would start the chase. We hardly went back to the motel alone. I was still single at that time, but Eddie was married and had a child. I was a little slow with the pickup lines, but I learned a lot from Eddie the charmer! We attended conventions and training sessions out of town together and no matter how raunchy our evenings were, we always were at the meetings right on time, drank as much mouth wash as scotch, I think. I could not believe that Eddie's wife never caught on to his infidelity. He was one hell of a salesman, so he really pulled the wool over her eyes for years. There was even one case of a possible paternity suit, but Eddie came out of that one without repercussion as well. Eddie used to say his vice was smoking but believe me chasing women was his forte. Like I said, I learned a lot from Eddie. I lost touch with him when he was promoted to management, I stayed in the same technical position until retirement.

John: Ed and I met at a Rotary luncheon, I knew of him and was familiar with some of his companies. We got talking about a new venture he had in advanced technology that was becoming very popular to businessmen and I was very impressed. I was invited to a house party he and his wife were throwing and attended. His friends and associates were all well-off successful men, and I was intrigued, we went outside to have a smoke and I asked him how I could get into a business like his. He jumped on the idea, we met in his posh office the next day and I committed to $10,000 for shares in a fledgling company that he said had great promise. I did not tell him that I would have to cash in our RRSPs to get the funds. Long story short, after many complicated explanations of how the idea fell short, I found out that I had been scammed, that bastard was so convincing. Ed said that investing was like baseball, you don't get a home run every time. If I had a baseball bat, I would have used it on him.

Fern: I met Ed when he was forty, he owned a company that was the same type of business that I was in, and we became partners. He was an impressive looking, accomplished businessman and I fell head over heels for him. We just clicked. I was divorced and he was ready to take that step. We started spending weekends together, and soon we couldn't bear to be apart. I was at his side in the businesses that he bought and sold after that, and we made a good team. He taught me a lot about business, and I taught him a lot about fidelity. We had a great life together travelling the world, skiing, golfing, visiting friends and family, and before we knew it, we were retired. He was very proud of the article that Jennifer Jones wrote about him in the Kelowna Tribune. But—that was then, and this is now!!!

FINAL CHAPTER

Ed *Hmm, what day is it today? Oh, yes, it is Monday, and I must go to a meeting of the board this morning. At the height of my career, I would have been looking for my cufflinks, but men don't wear them anymore. Tie clip – no longer necessary. Tie, hmmm I have many, do I want a narrow one or a wide one, stripes or plain, which one will make the best impression at this Board of Director's meeting? Ah, there are my brown oxfords 'Hey buddies, I missed you and you used to caress my feet all day. .... a* **successful man dresses the part.** *A three-piece suit and banker's brown shoes are sign of success.' I was a real looker wasn't I. Could have had my choice of ladies almost any time. I have had so many good years.*

Fern: Another Monday, and I am wondering what state of mind my beloved husband of 35 years would be in today. Ed was 78 years old, and until this year still extremely sharp. He has become very confused and troubled by it. He would come home late from a meeting and share the fact that he drove around looking for his favourite deli after the meeting, drove round and round looking for it, he wandered if the deli had moved location. He was confused in the meetings, thought the directors were all going off topic. The directors told me that Ed was very quiet and reserved in meetings, not the usual confident contributor of ideas that he used to be. Alpha Technologies took him off the board of directors which really confused Ed as he thought he was still a very valuable member. I started worrying about him and encouraged him not to drive anymore. I could drive him anywhere he wanted to go. This morning after his shower he got dressed for a business day. He stated how comfortable his banker's brown shoes still were, but I looked down and he was still in his slippers. I went to throw in a load of wash, and when I came upstairs, the front door was open, and the car was gone. The day was spent using all the resources I had to try to find him.

I don't know if it is fate or destiny but it doesn't seem fair that Eddie's greatest strength was his mind, and now it is his mind that is destroying him.

RCMP Member: "Sorry Ma'am, we haven't located your husband yet, we have an all points bulletin on the air and our members are searching for him. We are using the description of him and what he was wearing. No one has given us any clues yet. Can you please look at this slipper which we found on Highway 97 and the turnoff to Predator Ridge Golf Course, it seems to fit what you described? Yes, that is it, then I must inform you that your car was parked along that turnoff as well. We do not know if Ed went off on foot or was picked up by someone, we just have this slipper." OMG another Shoe on the Road Story.

RONNIE TO THE RESCUE

He was adopted shortly after he was born by the Williams family, and the only child the Williams had named him Ronnie. Tara loved Ronnie so much, she wanted him to sleep in her bed with her even though he had his own bed. Often, he was her baby, and she put a bonnet on him, and booties. He hated the booties and kicked them off immediately. She would put him in the baby stroller (the Williams had always wanted to have another child) and stroll him around the driveway, and as far as the mailbox if Mommy was with them.

When he got a little older, she would make him share in tea parties, and princess dances, and bedtime stories. Ronnie was the best playmate Tara ever had.

Tara did not like to eat broccoli, and when Mommy wasn't looking, she often tried to pass the broccoli on to Ronnie, but Ronnie didn't like broccoli either, so Tara always got caught and scolded.

Tara was a good pitcher, and she would throw the ball over and over again for Ronnie to catch. Ronnie loved playing ball with Tara and was disappointed when Mommy called them in for supper, he wanted to play ball until bedtime.

When Tara and Ronnie went for walks around the neighborhood, they often met other people out for a stroll. Tara was so proud when an old lady would comment on what beautiful big brown eyes Ronnie had. Ladies often asked how old he was, and Tara and Ronnie were always polite to them.

They visited Grandma and Grandpa's acreage often. Tara and Ronnie would head for the woods. Tara loved building forts and she was always the boss. She would tell Ronnie to get branches, and when he brought them, she would use them for the fort construction. No one worried about the two of them being in the woods alone. Tara was an independent young girl and wasn't a bit afraid that a cougar or a bear would appear in the woods behind Grandpa's shed. Ronnie was becoming Tara's protector and would not let anything hurt her.

The family often camped at Ellison Provincial Park, and Tara and Ronnie loved climbing the rocks by the beach. Today when they were on a climbing expedition, Tara slipped and fell off the rock trail and down about three feet onto a rock ledge below. Ronnie jumped down beside her and fretted that something had happened to Tara. Tara knew that her right foot was hurt badly, she tried to stand on it and couldn't put any weight on it. Tara started to cry and sat down in defeat, knowing that she could not climb back up to the trail. She took her runner off and massaged her ankle, *ouch – that was not a good idea*. Tara wanted to yell for Mommy and Daddy but knew they would not hear her at the campsite.

Ronnie knew just what to do. He grabbed Tara's runner and jumped up to the trail. With a backwards look to tell Tara everything would be alright, he headed to the campsite.

Daddy was chopping kindling for their evening fire, and when he saw Ronnie coming, he yelled for Mommy to come quickly, something had happened to Tara. He patted Ronnie on the head and said, "Good boy, Ronnie, show us where she is!!" as he took Tara's running shoe out of Ronnie's mouth.

Ronnie ran down the trail to Tara, she was still sitting on the rock and crying. Daddy lowered himself to the rock and lifted her into his arms, so happy to find her safe. Tara was so happy that she had her best friend Ronnie to rescue her, he was the best little dog ever. Thank goodness he didn't lose her shoe on the road.

Printed in Canada